Time Gentlemen

Published by

Percychatteybooks

ISBN 978 0 9954890 3 5

© Percy W Chattey 2016

Time Gentlemen

By

Percy W. Chattey

Percy is Five times Winner of the Pinnacle Book Achievement Award. He is also the only Author in twenty nine years, to have won two awards in a single session

'Time Gentlemen' won best adult fiction at the awards

As always for my lovely wife Jean,
friend and soul mate,
who has helped with the editing and all the rewrites,
whilst listening to all my ramblings
whilst putting this story together.

Also my appreciation to:
Derek Cook for the cover design
Chris Wyatt for his specialist help

*Other Thrilling Novels
From Percy*

Motorway

Humpty Majority Sat on the Wall

Who called Last Orders

Death for a Starter *(Best historical fiction)*

Living in Spain

Politicaly Incorrect *(Best Thriller)*

Dreams Lies Cheats & Reality

Blitz & Pieces *(Best Autobiography)*

The Black Venus *(Best Fiction)*

Watch*it!*

Watch*it Too!*

The Dauntless Factor

The Cormacks

My Friend Henry

Time Gentlemen *(Best Adult fiction)*

Characters

Aran Danoon	Mary is his wife
Bernard Walters	Paper shop man
Bill Perdway	Driver of dray lorry
Brian Arthur Roberts	Owner of Bar Games
Bobby	Bill Perdway's assistant
Burt & Irene Hallard	The Black Rose Landlords
Byron Smith	Detective Sergeant
Carol	Casino manager
Charlotte	Waitress & bar staff
Christopher Perkins	Boy friend of Liz Hallard
Dave Logan	Detective Sergeant
Declan O'Donnell	Terrorist leader
Dennis & Kay	Friends of Michael & June
Doris Gilding	Chairperson of the W.I.
Eddie	Irish terrorist
Frances Danoon	Aran & Mary's daughter
Ginger	Another name for Declan
George Pendleton	New Landlord Black Rose
Green	Detective Inspector
Harry Cox	Car salesman
Ian	Captain Parachute Regiment
Ivy Charlton	Jane's Mother

Jack Quincy	Waiter
Jane Charlton	Waitress daughter of Ivy
Jim	Landlord opening Chapter
June Whitehead	Wife of Michael
Kay	Wife of Dennis
Ken Williams	Part owner of Bar Games
Lewis	Irish terrorist
Liz Hallard	Burt & Irene's daughter
Margaret	Brewery assistant dispatcher
Michael	Husband of June
Mrs Perdway	Bill Perdways wife
Pam	Waitress & Paul's fiancé
Paul	Drummer and Pam's fiancé
Richard Donaldson	Store owner
Ron	Darts team treasurer
Sarah Roberts	Wife of Brian
Ted Walters	Brewery head dispatcher
Terry Parks	Head waiter
Tony	Irish terrorist
Vivian Dowling	Secretary Women's Institute

Forward

When terrorists use deadly violence, for the reason of some form of deep ideology, or revenge, it is to maim and annihilate the unsuspecting without any form of mercy.

Whereas the author does not wish to cause pain to families and kinsfolks who have had their lives totally changed because of an event, where loved ones have been destroyed whilst going about their daily routine, Percy feels this story should be told.

This tale whilst not true and purely imaginative mimics factual events where unsuspecting persons are involved in such a happening.

There are no chapters as the story is set in the same time zone.

Time Gentlemen

September 1949, Belfast, Northern Ireland

Early autumn, and the day is coming to a close. The late evening sun is spreading its red glow across the western skies of Belfast, promising a warm day for the morrow.

In the distance a ships siren splits the evening air with its mournful warning. The offices and factories, which make up the community of the Capital City of the British Province, start to close allowing their workers to leave so they could make their way home.

The numerous and varied bars are coming to life awaiting the evening revellers. As they arrive most of the talk is centred around the previous days Local Election, and the unexpected result which had ousted the previous Government, who had held office since the end of the Second World War, four years earlier.

The Catholic minority of the territory had resigned themselves to the new administration who now controlled the affairs of the community. Whilst most were prepared to accept the situation and lead a peaceful way of life, others were intent on stirring up trouble for their own political gain.

The early nineteen fifties saw the province with full employment and a robust future, although there was a long history of restlessness going back centuries causing a strong undercurrent of discontent, which some parties were trying to take advantage of.

Aran Danoon, lifted his glass and drained the last of his beer. Pushing himself away from the bar, he murmured his 'Goodbyes', having had his regular evening pint at the small back street public house close to the dock yard where he worked.

"Come on Aran, have another before you go home, it's about time you told that new wife of yours who's boss. Start as you mean to go on, that's what I always say."

The bar went quiet, Aran turned to look at the speaker, "Aye, and I suppose you would have me joining your Army, which I've told you before will only lead to trouble."

"Enough of that talk Aran, you know it cannot do any good. You used to be a useful man to have about, but now..." The speaker shrugged his shoulders allowing the words to die as Aran turned his back and purposefully made for the door.

Ginger, whose name was Declan O'Donnell, had been named after his grandfather who fifty years previously had been executed by the English for murdering two British soldiers. He had also been a senior member of the Irish uprising at that time, and now his grandson was determined to try and keep his memory alive.

Ginger and Aran had been friends since leaving school, and now his old friend wanted him to stay a little longer at the bar. But as it was not happening, he could feel his temper rising, as he was determined to bring the matter to a head.

Once they had been great buddies, but he had noticed a change in his old friend over the past few years. He turned and grabbed him by the arm, "Aran, why do we have to get bad tempered with each other every time we meet, you used to stay and have a good drink with the boys."

A hush had come over the bar, everybody knew what Ginger's temper was like and heads had turned to see what the harsh words were about. The Landlord stopped what he was doing and made his way over to the end of the bar where the flap was, which would allow him access into the room itself.

"Let go of my arm Ginger." Aran turned to look at his old friend.

"Why don't you stop for a while and have a drink with the lads?" he was staring the other in the face.

"I've told you not today, and I don't want to keep repeating myself every time I come in here."

"What are you frightened of Aran?" Abruptly Ginger, who was a big man, could feel himself getting irritated. Part of him wanted to drop the subject, however the more aggressive side of him was determined to change the others new ways since he had got wed.

"I'm not frightened of anybody, and you know it. I also know my Mary will be waiting for me at home, and she'll be wondering where I am." He took the others arm off his and turned again to go to the door.

Ginger, had seen the anger welling in Aran's eyes, he felt insulted and a little stupid, suddenly he knew he was making too much fuss, and yet somehow he felt it was important to try and change the others mind.

"You are becoming nothing but a coward Aran, and you don't care anymore for your fellow countrymen."

The word coward infuriated Aran, he turned completely round to face his old friend not caring that everyone was looking, although he did see the Landlord had lifted the flap on the bar and was making his way to the pair.

"You know I'm not a coward Ginger. You know that more than anyone, why did you want to call me things like that?" He took a firm grip of Declan's shoulder.

The Landlord, in a white shirt in contrast to the less than clean apron, stood next to them, "Come on lads, there's nothing to quarrel about, not in this house."

The two assailants took very little notice, both knowing that sometime there would have to be a showdown, and as both were angry with each other, the time seemed to be right for it to happen right there and then.

Ginger held up a hand putting it on the Landlord's chest, "Keep out of this Jim, we have got to settle this sometime."

The Landlord wanted to defuse the argument, as he was worried about the reputation of the Pub and any damage a fight would cause, and was trying to push his way in between them, "Come on lads, what is there to sort out?"

Aran had also put his free hand up, holding the Landlord back; facing up to Ginger and feeling himself going red and knowing that only a fight would settle the matter.

"I'll tell you what needs sorting out Jim, this big bloody oaf, who wants to tear the whole community apart with his united Ireland policy - he wants us all to be at war with the British. He wants us to fight each other in our own streets he..."

"That's enough of that Aran," suddenly Ginger felt himself remarkably calm which surprised him, he couldn't understand why he was not feeling angrier, normally by now he would have hit the other person.

"Your trouble is Aran, you have got yourself a job mixing with the natural enemy of Ireland and you have forgotten your friends."

"Ginger, you had better take that statement back about me being a coward, if not I'm going to crack your head wide open."

The Landlord stood looking from one to the other, sensing the tension between the two. He decided not to say anything as that may inflame the situation and he was hoping the whole thing would defuse itself between the two friends, whom he had known for many years.

Aran was still quivering with rage. His eyes were wide and he was snarling when he added. "What a lot of rot you talk, you know as well as I do that you could have started that work with me, if you hadn't been so full of your freedom for Ireland rubbish."

Ginger was derided by the statement, he could hardly believe his ears. Before Aran had got married the two of them had plotted and schemed, they had shared the same secrets, the same boyhood dreams. Now he realised that where he had believed in the cause his friend had not, and he had only been playing. He felt deceived and felt the blood rising in him.

The tension in the pub had started to relax after the initial argument, before anyone had noticed the new flashpoint, Ginger hit out.

Aran saw the punch coming at the same time that Jim realised Ginger was shaping up to hit out.

Before Aran could defend himself, the Landlord put up his hand to protect him, but only managed to hit him in the jaw. What happened next was not quite clear and was to become the subject of conversation for many months, what was clear Ginger was on the floor with Aran on top of him.

A space had cleared with the two men laying on the floor in the middle, the Landlord standing over them, both men stared at each other surprised at the turn of events.

"I'll say this once more Ginger, just once - you understand...I don't want to join your bloody Army, it will only lead to trouble, bad trouble, I'm quite happy, just leave me alone"

With that Aran, got up from the floor, pushing his way through the other regulars. At the door he turned and looked at his old friend and said "We are finished Ginger...finished!" he walked away allowing the door to shut on the closing unit, and made his way home.

"Mary, I'm home." Aran called, as he entered the hallway of the small terraced home that they had rented as newlyweds a few months earlier. Beyond the door was a tiny narrow passage leading through to the rear of the house where Aran could hear the sounds of cooking, also his wife's customary reply telling him that the evening meal would be ready in a few minutes.

Taking his jacket off he pushed his sleeves up and made his way to the kitchen sink, which was the only facility in the small cramped home. Picking up the soap he asked, "What sort of day you had, my love?"

She looked at him from dishing up the meal and smiling said "Boring! There is not a lot to do here, once I have swept around and dusted, and then that is it."

He turned and looked at her in surprise "Why's that?" there must be other things to keep you busy?"

"I miss the girls at the factory. Once you have gone off to work in the morning there's not a lot to do. The housework is soon finished, and then I have nothing to do for the rest of the day."

Mary stopped what she was doing and looking up at the man she loved asked in a simple way "Aran, please... why can't I go back to work?"

He spoke sternly "We have been through all that before, you know I will not have it, and when we have a family you will have enough to keep you busy then."

Mary knew it was of little use to argue with him, so she busied herself serving the evening meal, listening to him relay the day's events to her, finishing with the scene in the pub"

"Aran, I do wish you wouldn't mix with that crowd, they are up to no good, and it can only lead to trouble." She had started to clear the empty plates.

"Aye, you could be right, that's what I told them tonight, perhaps I'll have me drink in another pub on the way home, there's a place where some of the other lads go to from work, that's where I'll go tomorrow night."

"If you must have a drink on your way home, then I would prefer it if you did that - at least you wouldn't be mixing with that other crowd."

~~~

Although the desire for a family was strong, and being devout Catholics, no precautions were ever taken to prevent children, it was to be another four years before Mary discovered she was pregnant. By then she had returned to the work she had been employed at before she was married, getting her own way after eighteen months of gently nagging. As time passed and there was no sign of a family being started, Aran relented and a week later Mary started where she had left off.

The couple were besides themselves with joy at the news. What neither of them knew was that nature had performed one of its miracles, and the night they had united in love, the egg inside Mary, on being fertilised split into two and formed identical girl twins. From birth their indistinguishable looks, manners and ways confused everyone, and whilst Mary would never admit it, she herself had difficulty in seeing the unique difference between the two.

Frances

The twins, Josephine and Frances, frequently shortened to Josie and Fran, were in their second year at Junior school when the first bombs went off in Belfast, heralding the start of a new reign of terror in the province.

The two girls had adjusted to an atmosphere of violence and hatred, whilst their parents tried to give them a normal up bringing by trying to isolate them from the troubles that were going on around them.

The task was an impossible one, the nightly crump as bombs exploded throughout the troubled city, the gunfire and violence in the street were all sights and sounds that could not be hidden from the youngsters.

As the situation deteriorated on a daily basis, the English Government was concerned and ordered the Army to intervene. The arrival of British soldiers on the streets, the inevitable sandbags and check points, whilst helping to minimise the fighting, did nothing to encourage the upbringing of the two girls.

As the state of affairs worsened, the city became bomb scarred, with whole streets raised to the ground. Factories were destroyed creating a spiral in the unemployment rate, which forced people out of work and into a life of frustration, and easy recruitment into the various political groups that were emerging and were at war with each other.

Mary and Aran had often spoken on moving although never making a decision - always hoping that tomorrow would bring news of an end to the fighting and a settlement to bring the province back to normal. Instead each day brought new killings or maiming, more ugliness and hope fading.

Despite everything the two girls were happy and continued to take advantage of their likeness, confusing people they met and sometimes their own parents.

The family was very close and despite the troubles in the neighbourhood, they were happy, almost as if they were an island untouched by the civil war that raged all around them.

Disaster struck one warm Sunday, that was to be known in the future as 'Bloody Sunday'. Although the family had deliberately not got involved in the troubles, on that particular day it was impossible to avoid the confrontation that some hard-core troublemakers were determined to create with the police and the Army.

The area close to their home became a battle ground. The front windows had been smashed and for safety the family took shelter in the rear of the house.

During a period when the fighting appeared to have moved away from their house, Aran went through to the front of the dwelling, returning shortly after to retrieve his coat, stating that one of their neighbours was lying hurt in the road and that he was going out to help him.

Despite his wife's pleading he was determined to go, and left by the front door. As he closed it behind him she ran to the windows overlooking the thoroughfare, the girls following her and holding each other were peering over her shoulder. They were in time to see a unit of the Army chasing a gang into the street, followed by gun fire.

Aran had reached the helpless man and was leaning over to help him - abruptly he spun round, as a bullet hit him, and he fell heavily.

From where the girls stood, they could see the blood spreading across the rear of his jacket. Mary screamed and ran for the front door. The twins filled with fear for their father stayed at the window; the event they were watching creating a picture which was perpetually traced on their minds.

Thirteen people died that day. The red head gear of the Paratroop Regiment, which was the unit that had been mainly involved, received most of blame as to how the situation was handled.

Later it was established that it was an Army bullet that had killed Aran. The I.R.A. pressed home it's advantage on the twins, taunting them with what the Forces had done, breeding hate, to create more hate to further their own cause with two new recruits.

The twins sixteenth birthday was approaching, despite the loss of the previous year, they were determined to make it a 'swinging affair'. They had both grown into beautiful identical young ladies; inseparable, confusing and mystifying the world in their likeness.

They had planned a party, which was to be held in the living room of the small terraced house, that had once stood in a street of similar neat homes. However, the troubles had left their mark, numerous houses stood gutted where fire bombs had been thrown through windows. Some of them had the buildings on each side, severely damaged by bombs, which had been used against the dwellings.

It was springtime and the day was bright and warm. The two girls were in their last year at school, and were making their way home, laughing at their own silly jokes. If they had been looking, they would not have known who the person was standing in an alleyway as they passed; they certainly would not have taken any notice of him. Nonetheless, he recognised them, as he had been waiting for them. On the other hand, the twins did see the British Army patrol in front of them, beyond their own turning and some way down the street, which in itself was not an unusual sight to see servicemen patrolling the area.

They had almost reached the corner, where they would turn down, their home a mere fifty yards away. Behind them the man now wearing a hood stepped out from the alleyway to the rear of them raising his rifle and pointing it at their backs. The twins could not see what the terrorist was doing but they did see the first soldier, drop to one knee raising his rifle pointing it in their direction. The violent noise of gunfire, instantly shattering the afternoon's tranquillity, as the shockwaves echoed around the scarred streets.

Michael & June – Dennis & Kay

A young couple in their early thirties pulled into the car park of The Black Rose. Michael, who was a stocky man wearing grey slacks with a black jacket and an open neck white shirt, pointed to a blue Austin Maxi car saying "Well it looks like they are here."

June smiled nervously "I suppose now we are here, we had better go in, how are they going to know us ... although I think I would much prefer to go home?"

"I know how you feel but I think we should carry on, if we don't like them then we could always leave"

He looked at his wife, she saw he had a sickly smile on his face and knew by his actions he was looking forward to meeting this couple, who they had only spoken to on the phone.

He continued "I told him the make and model of our car and he said he would keep a look out for it."

"Alright, as they will already know we are here I suppose we had better go and find them ... but if I don't like the look of him then we are leaving straight away." He nodded mumbling 'Okay' as he opened the door of the Ford Cortina.

Dennis, a tall slim man with a scruffy mop of blond hair, although immaculately dressed in a casual way, was the total opposite of Junes husband. He was true to his word and was waiting in the foyer standing near the doorway as the pair entered the building.

Holding out his hand he introduced himself saying his wife Kay, was in the restaurant waiting at a table. Michael shook his hand and exchanged pleasantries with him.

June was stunned by his soft gentle, yet firm voice and was aware of him sweeping his eyes over her as if he was removing her garments, although in reality he was only removing her outer coat, while her husband stood and watched.

At first, with mixed feelings and determined to feel positive although she thought she should feel revulsion for him. Instead her feelings were the complete opposite. When his eyes returned to her face and looked into hers, she felt weak at the knees, her heart hammering in her chest.

He took her hand to shake it and June then knew she was going to enjoy the rest of the evening, and was starting to look forward to it, although she was not sure she could take her clothes off or let this new friend fondle her.

They entered the large room, her first reaction was to the soft music playing. Looking to her left to see where it was emanating from she saw a small stage with three musicians in concert, the tinkling of a piano to the fore performing the latest popular tunes. They made their way through the noise and chatter to the eating area.

June had immediately noticed the woman sitting by herself who was waving her hand at them, they made their way through to where she was sitting. She stared at her husband and saw the gleam in his eyes as he saw Dennis's wife and knew instantly they were not going to leave, as the look of the other woman was portraying sex. A little blond dressed in a lacy black costume with a very short skirt and low neckline, which made her feel a little dowdy, when comparing her own attire to Dennis's wife.

The new man who had just entered her life took control of the seating arrangements as he held out a chair for her, helping her into it by holding her waist and managing to touch her breasts as he did so. He pulled out the adjoining seat next to her and sat down.

She looked across the table and saw her husband ogling Kay, and whilst excited she could not help wondering how she had let herself agree to such an evening. But she could not escape the feeling of sexual undertones.

She looked at Dennis, whom she expected to be her partner for the evening, and let the thought come into her head of what his slim body was like, and his manhood. Was it strong and hard? She blushed at the thought.

As the evening progressed, the four became very friendly and chatted freely as if they had known each other for a very long time.

It came as a shock to June when she realised that they had naturally paired off with their opposite partners and she felt comfortable watching her husband flirting with the other woman. Wasn't she doing the same?

The meal came to an end and they ordered brandies and cocktails. As the waiter, who had served them walked away, June felt Dennis's hand on her leg, he was saying something about blue movies.

She looked around her in embarrassment, to see if anyone was listening and had heard what he had said, at the same time she pushed his hand away from her thigh. Unexpectedly she had a feeling of trepidation for the rest of the evening.

Frances

In the Northwest corner of Wales is the Isle of Anglesey with the port of Holyhead at its furthest point. An early morning sea mist swirling in from the water had made the dockside damp and clammy.

Its emptiness of an hour earlier was now filled by the British Rail Dublin ferry that had, despite its size, slipped into the water's edge. The flotsam forced into the narrow gap as the monster, home safe from the sea, came to its berth.

A dockside that had been empty except for cargo, stacked like dark deserted fortresses in the gloom of the sea front, was now a hive of activity as stevedores, dock workers and railwaymen prepared to unload the morning arrival.

Further back alongside the quay, past the Customs and Immigration officers, the first train of the day, an express for Euston Station, waited for the passengers from the ferry to board it, before taking its long dash through the early morning countryside to the Capital City of London.

At the rear of the train the mail bags from Ireland and other packages and luggage were being loaded. Whilst that activity was going on the first of the passengers from the ship walked down the platform, beside the stationary train selecting carriages, the odd door being slammed shut. Whilst at the front, the deep throb of the locomotive's diesel engine could be heard, as the engineer made ready for the coming journey.

Special Branch and Security men, sitting at a desk and studying the passengers as they passed, had recognised a few travellers, some known to be involved in a terrorist organisations whilst others were identified to have sympathy to their cause, although not known as active extremists. Their movements to and from Northern Island was watched with interest and duly noted.

In the column of people nobody paid much attention in the poor lighting to the girl in her late teens, dressed in a long dark skirt and duffle coat, her hair shoulder length, like a dark hood framing her face.

Only a few of her fellow passengers had noticed the deep set eyes that did not smile, despite her youthfulness and radiant cheeks. Most of the people who tried to talk to her had found her difficult to correspond with, the glazed look, hiding a hatred that only she understood.

Keeping herself to herself, she sat in the corner of a second class carriage and waited patiently for the train to start the journey, which would take her to a city that she had only read about, but where she knew there would be friends waiting to welcome her, and to help her in her cause.

The compartment filled with other souls, all going their own way. And yet to Frances Danoon, they did not exist as her mind was back two years before, when at the age of sixteen, she along with her twin sister Josephine, walked home laughing and joking from the local library in their hometown of Londonderry. Books under arms they were excited about their birthday the following day and the friends who had been invited to tea.

As sisters they were very close. Their twin births and the following loving upbringing by devoted parents, creating a bond between them. A bond only they could understand, one that stretched beyond the normal human relationship and understanding, a union that only the intimacy of twins accepted as part of themselves, something real to be treasured and nurtured.

The train gave a small jolt, as the powerful engine encased inside the locomotive picked up speed as the engineer fed more fuel into the engine, finally setting the train into motion. The silver tracks reflecting what poor lighting there was, started to slide under the numerous wheels that were going to carry the passengers and luggage at high speed to the Capital.

Frances was looking out of the fast moving train, her reflection thrown back at her as the carriages hurtled through a tunnel. As she looked at herself she could see her sister's face, the laughter as they talked and joked and the agony of that fateful day all those years before.

They were so near to home, only one corner to turn and they would be in their street. When with suddenness, and from close at hand, came the shock of a rifle being discharged. Not an unfamiliar sound in this troubled district. But its closeness and the violence of the noise, had appeared to have come from behind them. However, they could only see the soldiers pointing their guns in what appeared to be their direction.

Both girls started to run, home was so near. Then there was another shot followed by a volley Frances remembered vividly the hand that was holding hers tightening, her sister stumbled and fell, blood gushing from her mouth, her lips distorted in pain. She felt a pain in her own shoulder, but her concern for her twin pushed it out of her mind. Across the street not far away soldiers were running, rifles held in their hands, she knew before kneeling beside the form on the ground that Josie was dead.

She hugged her, her blood staining and going through her own clothes. She heard people running towards her, screaming, a police siren or was it an ambulance, it was all too late the one person she lived for was dead in her arms, and the Army was at fault.

She was determined to have revenge. How? She did not know. She became more aware of the pain she herself had, trying to push it into the back of her mind, looking at her dead sister promising her that she would repay the debt.

It was weeks before she came out of hospital and by then, so many other tragedies had occurred that her experience was just another dead headline. She found it tough and demanding to adjust to life without her beloved twin sister, she was lonely, finding other people difficult to get on with.

The inquest findings were that a terrorist organisation had killed her sister. She was told that Josie had been deliberately murdered, by a protestant group fighting to do away with the Catholics.

She dismissed the findings of the inquest and the statement put out by the Army. She had seen the soldiers on the fateful day and was not going to be deterred from the revenge that burned deeply in her heart.

It had not been long afterwards that she had been approached by the I.R.A. and recruited to their ranks as an active member. From time to time she was contacted and as the movement recognised the hatred that burned inside her, knew they would be able to use it for their own purposes.

Although she craved for action, she was ordered to wait. And as one year passed and another began her hatred deepened so every day it consumed her more deeply. Just when her patience was running out, she received word that she was to go to London, to an address in Holloway where she would be contacted.

The train had pulled into Euston Station after an uneventful journey spilling its tired passengers out on to the platform. On leaving the comfort of the carriage Frances was confused as to where to go and was overwhelmed by the intensity of the crowd.

After a short journey on the Underground Railway, having first worked out its complexities, Frances found herself standing on the doorstep of a rundown Victorian building, in a back street off the Holloway Road in North London.

An elderly Irish woman ushered her up the stairs in silence, showing her into a small room at the back of the house that had a huge ceiling making the room look tall and narrow. From the draughty sash type window, she could see the backs of identical houses in the road running parallel, the back gardens an assortment of rubbish dumps, neat and mowed lawns with vegetable patches and others just a jumble of weeds.

The room was sparsely furnished and not very homely, nevertheless feeling very tired, and as soon as the old lady had left her, she lay on the single bed, which was against the wall. She was dozing when a phone somewhere in the house started to ring, ignoring it she slipped into a deep sleep, the weariness of the journey catching up with her.

Burt & Irene

A gust of wind played with the waste paper in the emptying car park, unfilled crisp bags, peanut packets along with other discarded wrappers and cigarette packs, made a whirling pattern caught like trapped shadowy pagan dancing figures in the orange floodlight mounted on the adjoining public house.

The outside neon signs above the 'Black Rose', declaring Casino and Restaurant in bright coloured illumination, were, along with the other lighting going out one at a time, creating deeper shadows, as the last of the customers spilled out into the chilled night air.

People in groups, pairs or singularly, making their own way to their abodes or other pleasures in the remaining hours of the evening. The public bar had closed for the day, leaving a few clients finishing their meals in the restaurant. Double doors separated it and the adjoining large saloon and lounge bar, which doubled as a reception area. At one end on the small stage, facing the tables and immediately behind the small dance floor, played a three piece band, the music soft and low, matching the mood of the patrons that were left.

In the saloon bar the Landlord was clearing away the final glasses, which the staff had been collecting and cleaning, whilst his wife undertook a similar task in the public bar which was designed so that the two serving areas were adjacent to each other.

Burt Hallard looked up from his task and glanced over at his wife Irene, "Not a bad night." He said more out of habit than a statement of fact before returning to the task of making the area ready for the following day.

There was a small pause before she replied, "Yes, I thought we were in for a little bit of trouble at one time though...honest love, I don't know why you let that bunch into the place, they are not the sort we really want in the building."

"I don't know - just because a couple are Irish, it does not mean to say they are bad, maybe a bit high spirited, but nothing more. Anyway, we will be gone in a few months and then we won't have to worry."

"But you never used to think like that. Did you see in the papers what the IRA did to those two pubs? Blew them to bits with the people still inside, and one of them is not far from here. It wasn't long ago when you would have barred them without a second thought."

"Aye, perhaps love, maybe I'm getting too old for this game, anyway as I was saying we will be gone in a few months, and our new place will be a lot easier to manage and will suit us until we reach our retirement. And then we will be rid of the routine and will be able to do what we wish."

"You may be right, I don't suppose we want any trouble now, not after all these years. But when the two Irish started to have a stand up argument with the regulars I just thought we should have done something" Not being able to see the restaurant from where she was standing, she paused before, adding, "Is the restaurant empty yet?"

Pam one of the bar staff answered for him "No, not yet, there's just one table, it looks like they are just finishing now." She had hardly finished speaking when the band stopped playing and started to pack away their instruments with accomplished skill. Paul the drummer gave a small wave to Pam who smiled back at him.

~~~

Outside in the car park the two Irishmen were talking "As I told you Ginger, it is the ideal place especially as the Army are frequent visitors."

"You are not going to do much damage with a car loaded with explosives; the place is far too large – what's your plan?"

"A device planted in the cellars, I am thinking in terms of a beer keg and some form of timer."

"I follow what you are saying Tony, and sounds as if it could work." They both walked deep in thought over to where their car was parked. Declan O'Donnell broke the silence "I will need to get approval, in the meantime look into the possibility of how to obtain the beer kegs – and how you are going to deliver them into the cellars."

"I have done some research into that part already – when shall we meet again, I can explain then?"

Declan started the engine of the car "I'll go back to Ireland, I do not see there will be a problem of getting authority for what you are suggesting, so let's meet back here in ten days time. I think we should put a suit on, and we will have dinner in the restaurant."

~~~

The two couples at the table stood up and Dennis took hold of June's hand, walking over to retrieve her coat, which he had previously hung on a coat hanger, giggling and laughing as they did so. The staff heard one of the women say," I'll go with Michael in his car, we don't live too far from here."

There were nods and agreements as they slowly made their way to the door. Burt waited until they had left the premises before following and shutting the door firmly behind them, pushing the security bolts home.

He straightened himself and looked around the plush furnishings of the saloon, with one of the staff polishing the last table. The emptiness after a night of laughter, music and noise always seemed unnatural, the bareness created by the licensing laws of the land, and not by the wishes of those that had been present.

Burt made his way across the carpeted floor to the bar where he asked the staff if they wanted their normal good night drink.

The sudden clash of a symbol from the band that played on a regular basis was an unnatural noise amongst the tinkering of the glasses and the bottles as Burt poured the drinks. There was a curse accompanying the sound as Paul stooped to retrieve the instrument.

Behind the bar the landlord switched the extractor fans off, the humming that had not been noticed until that moment, left an eerie quietness to the premises. Voices were hollow in the vastness of the bar.

With the evenings work completed, the staff and members of the trio, gathered around for their habitual good night drink before going home. They spoke in lowered tones weary after the day's activities.

Paul, the leader of the group of musicians, put his arm around Pam's shoulder, who worked part time behind the bar, when the group were playing. The governor looked over at them, "How long before the pub loses you two?" His voice carried no hostility; it was more like a father concerned about his chicks going out in the world.

"Four weeks tonight and we will be starting our honeymoon. That will also be the first night with the new Landlords" Paul replied, "Anyway, the pub won't be losing us for quite a while yet, there's a lot of things to buy, so we will be needing all the money we can lay our hands on."

Charlotte, the youngest of the group laughed, "Well then, where's the honeymoon going to be?"

"None of your business," Pam retorted, "Anyway, I don't even know the answer to that question." She hugged Paul around the waist as she spoke, looking into his face as she finished the sentence.

"Don't blame you love, don't let anybody know. I can remember when Burt and myself were married..." Irene was on one of her reminisces, the remainder of the party, nodded dutifully, but nobody really listened as the monologue was boring, the story old and by experience the listeners knew they would not be able to get a word in. So they stood and listened, drank their drinks and waited for the opportunity to escape.

Michael & June – Dennis & Kay

The Austin Maxi car lowered itself down the slope from the car park of The Black Rose into the road. June gave an involuntary shiver, from the cold that had got at her, through her flimsy top and skirt, despite the top coat she had draped around her shoulders, before getting into the car. The engine had not warmed up enough for the heating to work and she felt chilly and uncomfortable.

There were deep shadows and brightly lit areas in the car, coming from the headlights of her husband's Ford Cortina, which was immediately behind them. Briefly the street lighting reflected from the windscreen on to her companions' face. She tried to see his expression, but it was nothing she could read.

Turning to her own thoughts, she wondered, as she had many times that evening, how she had allowed herself to get into this situation, and with some trepidation about how the remainder of the evening would progress.

For fifteen years she and Michael had been what she would have called 'Happily married'. They had raised three normally healthy children, bought their own home and were respected amongst their immediate neighbours and peers.

It had come as a big shock to realise that her partner was not happy. At first, he had started to bring home, and read, explicit men's magazines displaying nude women. Then he had become more demanding. She had found it difficult to respond which had led to the start of many arguments.

All the time they had known each other they had never talked about sex. She had let him take the initiative, lying back as a dutiful wife, whilst he finished. She could not understand what had happened to have changed him. What had made him more demanding? She saw her wedded bliss being threatened. So she had tried to change to match his new thoughts.

One night he had been reading some of the more sexual booklets that he had been bringing home, which left her slightly cold and a little disgusted. In almost desperation she was trying to match his mood, drinking heavily to see if she could rid herself of the guilt feeling that lingered in her.

Now, in the car, she remembered the evening clearly. The children were tucked up in bed, she was lying on the settee trying to understand her feelings and get excited for Michael at the same time. He was sitting in a chair reading, occasionally he would chuckle, then he spoke, "There's a couple here that want to meet another swinging couple. Shall we answer it and see what happens?" He had looked across at her with a grin on his face.

At first she did not know what to say. She had never been unfaithful to Michael in all the years she had known him. The thought had never seriously crossed her mind. And now here he was suggesting it. Despite the initial revulsion, she found the idea slightly exciting and the more she thought about it, the more the idea appealed to her, especially if it pleased her husband and perhaps then they could get back to how they used to be.

She had looked up at him and studied his face to see if he was serious, and June realised he was. It was not until after the small advertisement had been answered, and the cold reality of the following day, did she start to have regrets, of which there were many.

Nevertheless, she had been determined to go through with it, although hoping Michael would have a change of heart, but he had not. And now here she was sitting in a strange car, with a man she had only met a few brief hours before, although she found herself attracted to this beautifully dressed person who had a positive and determined attitude, quite the opposite to Michael who was a little dowdy and old-fashioned and being employed at the same place since he had left school.

"You are deep in thought ... don't you like me?" The words were spoken softly, hardly audible over the noise of the car.

At first, she was not certain if he expected a reply or not. She was not going to tell him what her thoughts were, and no way was she going to burnish his ego, he had enough of that anyway. She looked at him and felt a pleasant sensation of some form of need sweeping through her. June decided to answer with a question "How far to your house?" she also managed a smile while saying it.

"Not far, just around that next corner on the right." The words hung in the air before he added in the form of a question "Nervous?"

In the dim light of the car he looked down at the hem of her frilly skirt barely reaching to her knees, with the hint of an undergarment below. Her legs were stretched out in front of her seat encased in sheer black nylon stockings hinting at hidden pleasures. A sexual buzz swept through him as he thought of the wonder above them, and would it be his tonight.

"It all seems soo...so...cold and sordid..." She stuttered her voice trailing off like a little girl. Although deep down she knew she only felt that way because she would much prefer it if they were alone and did not have to share the evening with her husband. She was wondering what would happen would all four of them be on the same bed at the same time, the thought made her go cold.

"Don't worry, it won't be. We will all get a little relaxed and see what happens. You know you are really a very lovely lady." He looked at her smiling, trying to reassure her, feeling activity in his jeans.

His words sent a feeling of delight through her. Although a feeling of panic started to well up inside her. June wanted to escape - she did not want Michael to see her with him, as she wanted it to be something special. He had returned his eyes to the road as she looked at him. Unexpectedly, a thought struck her and she said firmly "We are not going to take drugs or anything, are we...?" She had wanted to add his name but it had vanished from her mind.

He laughed "No! Nothing like that, just old fashioned drink, while we watch a blue movie." He took one hand from the steering wheel, giving hers a small squeeze.

She found his touch warm and inviting. She liked the feel of it and held it tightly. She said, "We have – well at least, I have never seen a..." June had found it difficult to say 'blue movie' "are they very suggestive?"

"We have a couple, both exciting to watch, one of which has two young girls in skimpy nurses uniforms undressing a man and pleasuring him, very exciting – you would look great in one of those, uniforms I mean not movies – but then again you would look great in both."

They drove on in silence, her nerves in a tangle a feeling of excitement cursing through her. June heard him say "Here we are now." The car had stopped in the short drive of a detached bungalow that looked like so many others in the road. In many ways it was not dissimilar to the one she herself lived in.

She found herself calming down, although now it was time to leave the comfort of the vehicle, and move on to the next phase, where she knew she was going to feel the strangeness of another man close to her and perhaps the ultimate coupling. June was excited and yet dreading getting out of the car.

She waited and watched with admiration as Dennis left the car and walked round it. Her door opened. She looked up at him standing there. Her thoughts had been trying to come to terms with the situation, would they just have a drink and watch blue movies. She saw her husband's Cortina pull into the kerb with another woman sitting in her seat, beside him. Would the men take it in turns with the females, she did not think she could cope with that?

It all seemed unreal, the glow from the streetlights reflecting through the trees lining the thoroughfare, giving a ghostly and dreamlike appearance.

As both his hands reached out for hers to help her out of the car – for some reason his action felt so natural one of being courted.

She took them, they felt warm, feeling excitement replacing the fear, knowing as she got out of the car and entered his home, there would be no return.

She sat for a moment looking up at him standing in front of her. She let her eyes stray over him once again feeling the pull of him and she knew it was going to be fun to go to bed with him, and if it did not happen then she was going to be very disappointed.

Pushing the doubts and uncertainties to the back of her mind, smiling she turned on the seat and put both legs on the ground. He was still holding her hands and with a gentle tug pulled her upright.

June stood up pecking him on the lips, whispering, "Let's go inside Dennis." His name came to her, as if she had never forgotten it.

Paul & Pam

The side door of the 'Black Rose' opened, Paul accompanied by Pam, were the first to escape Irene's continuous nattering. They strolled away from the pub, their hands entwined, oblivious to the world and its surroundings. What few people were about looked and smiled and remembered the days when they were in love.

The young couple, neither of them had any brothers or sisters, had known each other from junior school days. Pam's father was in the clergy and her mother was a devout Christian, with a strict view on life, both had brought their daughter up with decency and modesty.

"Darling, we are going the wrong way, I live in that direction." Pam pointed with her free hand the path they should be taking to her home.

He turned with pleading eyes "I thought we should just pop round to the flat, to make sure everything is alright."

Her laughter was like music to his ears, "Darling, I don't think that is the real reason at all." Her eyes flashed at him. "In fact, I know very well what you want, and I've already told you, the first time you get me on that brand new bed will be on our wedding night." She put her arm around his waist reassuringly, pulling him to her, and felt the comfort of his arm across her shoulder as he leant over to kiss her.

"I promise you love, we won't even go near the bedroom. But I think we should check just in case thieves have broken in." He was nibbling her right ear as he spoke.

Pushing him away, she quietly but firmly said "No." he stood with a hurt look on his face. She took him in her arms kissing him. "Darling, it is not that I don't want to. I love our little flat and I think we are lucky to have it. And I love our furniture and everything. But darling, it is not too long to wait...and then..." she trailed off not letting the words come out. He turned and started walking in the direction of their respective homes.

"Darling, you are not mad at me?" She was looking up into his face.

"No...just a need for you, a need to show my love – that's all." The music of her laughter could be heard echoing around the street before he continued "Before I sold the car, to buy furniture for the flat, at least I could say good night to you properly.

"I know darling. Honestly, I do want you so much but please let us wait – it is not too long now." Having got her own way she took hold of his hand. Not much more was said on the way to her house, both feeling that something, albeit very small, had been lost, in reality only a portion of a dream had been chipped away.

Burt & Irene

Burt ushered Irene up the wide staircase to the upper floor of the 'Black Rose.' She went into the small kitchen to make their customary cup of coffee, which they would drink in the adjoining comfortable lounge before going to bed.

"You know love, I'm getting too old for a place this size, I'm glad we will be moving in a few weeks. I'm also pleased we told the regulars, I felt bad about deserting them after all these years."

His wife continued to make the 'instant' coffee not making any comment as they had been over the same conversation many times.

He continued "I'm sure we are doing the right thing, the new place is tiny compared to The Black Rose, and it will be so much easier to handle. If we stay there for about five years we should have enough to retire on and be reasonably comfortable."

"Yes, I know love; we have been over it so many times." She brought the drinks into the living area, "I think the customers are planning something – I heard Mary..."

He looked at her a smile hovering around his lips "Which one is Mary?" Burt interrupted.

"The dark haired girl, always wearing slacks when a skirt would suit her much better – comes in with her husband, I think he's a lorry driver or something – comes into the Public Bar in overalls name of Ron..."

Burt was nodding his head "Yes, I know who you mean."

"Well I was standing behind the bar and Mary had her back to me – she was talking to the blond girl and she mentioned about us going and had they...that is the friends they were with...made up their minds what they were going to do – then one of them noticed me and they hushed up. I pretended not to hear."

He was looking at her with a puzzled look on his face "What do you think she meant?"

"Well, it was obvious they were talking about us leaving, and giving us something before we go. Apparently, they want to keep it a secret so we will have to wait and see."

Burt chuckled more to himself than anything "Oh, I'll be bowled over, I wonder what it will be; it is a nice thought whatever it is. It is going to be a great evening I got a message today to say that the Managing Director of the Brewery wants to be here, and they are making arrangements through the new manager who takes over the following day. I feel a little left out of the planning for our last evening here."

"Never mind love, I'm sure it will all work out fine."

Burt was about to get out of his seat when he said, "By the way love, who was the fellow walking around with a millboard in his hand this morning?"

"He said he was from the Estates Office at the Brewery and wanted to carry out an inspection of the property. I wandered around with him for a little while and when I told him I was too busy to follow him about all day, he suggested I was to leave him alone – so I did."

"What was he looking for, do you know?"

"I don't know and I am not certain he knew although he seemed efficient enough making sketches, especially in the cellar he seemed very interested down there."

"My guess, is that seeing we are leaving, the Brewery want to make sure everything is as it should be. And I suppose the cellars are important as they support the whole building."

Irene looked at the mantle clock and got up from her chair saying "Come on Burt, it is time for bed."

Michael & June – Dennis & Kay

The main lights in the Langton's living room were turned down very low, with only two table lamps, one at each end of the lounge throwing a warm orange glow across the ceiling and throughout the room, which was divided by an arch that had originally been a wall separating two different areas.

A soft stereo sound reverberated through the room the melody could be clearly heard, which relayed from a music centre, spreading a diffused glow from its control lights, in one corner of the room.

On arriving the four of them had enjoyed a drink together sitting around a polished table, with the two men eagerly looking at their partner for the evening in undisguised passion. Dennis had wasted no time in setting up a projector and a tall white screen on a stand.

The two ladies were dressed for the occasion in obvious sexual outfits both with low neck lines, although June's was nowhere near as daring as her new friend. Kay, a small slim blond with long curly hair, was looking stunning in a revealing black lacy suit, with an exceptionally short skirt, the top of which showed the swell of her breasts. She was totally relaxed, smiling and laughing occasionally at the conversation, her eyes darting frequently at Michael.

June was a little nervous, so much so, that Dennis, not knowing how she felt was not sure if she would agree to the eventual separation and the following event. She was dressed in the fashion of the day with a flared skirt over layers of petticoats her blouse transparent enough to show her black bra beneath.

With the clink of glasses, she dragged her eyes back to her partner for the evening; he was standing at a cabinet pouring another drink.

She looked at his back, his blond hair and she had a warm feeling of wanting to rub her hands through it. The excitement in the pit of her stomach edging her on - yet rationally she told herself that she should insist on being taken straight home. She wondered where the keys to their car were, perhaps in Michael's jacket which was hanging on the back of a chair.

Dennis placed a fresh drink in front of her and turned to the projector and set the film in motion. As the titles started to flash across the screen, the two couples made themselves comfortable on two settees, and settled down to watch the film.

Two scantily dressed young women appeared on the film, June watched in awe as the story progressed.

She watched with excitement flowing through her as they stroked and kissed whilst rubbing their bodies over a man, who was lying down, and they were slowly removing his clothing.

With her heart thumping and her breasts tingling, she watched as the two girls started to take it in turns to pleasure the male

She took another fleeting glance down the far side of the room; her husband was in a deep embrace, his hand sliding up the girls' leg pushing her skimpy skirt even higher, revealing the top of her stockings held up by a suspender belt, as they sat closely together watching the action taking place on the blue movie.

June's partner had stood up to refresh their glasses once more. She followed him, as she had seen enough of the film, standing close to him putting her hand on his hip.

A drink was put in her hand, she turned her head looking up into Dennis's eyes. She was wondering what it would feel like, when, as she knew he would, start to explore her body. She felt a tingle of expectation flow through her.

Taking the glass she smiled up at him their eyes flirting with each other's. The feeling in each, of being trapped inside a cocoon and nothing else mattered. He touched his glass to hers while looking down the front of her blouse feeling eagerness cursing through him. He was certain her attitude was changing as she seemed more relaxed.

She looked down and could see the bulge in the front of his tight denim jeans and she felt the need in her, she had a feeling of wanting to touch it, but declined. His drink was in one hand the amber liquid rocking to and fro. He leant forwards his lips were warm and welcoming as they touched hers.

June felt the slight pressure of his tongue. He slid his free hand around her neck gently pulling her to him they stood as one, each with a glass in one hand their mouths locked at the same time. They both put their glasses down in unison as if by some hidden message.

It was not long before she felt Dennis's hand roaming over her body, sliding up beneath her blouse and cradling her breasts.

"Shall we go somewhere we can be alone?" His eyes were pleading with hers. She picked up her tumbler from the small table – she shook her head "Not yet, I may need this." She was smiling as she lowered her eyes, mesmerised by that lump, which she had a strong desire to hold. Looking back up at his face smiling and took a sip of the fiery liquid.

Taking her free hand, he led her across the carpeted room and through a door into a bedroom. Glancing over her shoulder she could see her husband following Kay, who was now only wearing her underwear, into another room.

For one brief moment she jealously admired the shape of the other woman, she was so slim, possibly a size thinking *she could not remember being that small?'* Abruptly she did not care, she felt good and knew she looked it. And now, what she had been looking forward to with trepidation, was about to happen.

The room was not very large, long mirrored wardrobes giving the impression it was greater than it was. At first it seemed the bed, which was reflected in the glass, appeared to take up the whole of the space like a sacrificial altar, and she was the sacrifice.

She could smell his aftershave as he took the drink from her hand and laid it on the side table.

June was standing in front of him their eyes playing games with each other as they were locked together.

June reached up undoing the buttons on his shirt. Very slowly, one at a time. She pulled the garment out of his jeans and pushed it back off his shoulders.

Her whole body came alive as anticipation and fear flowed through her as she watched him starting to undo the belt at his waist. In matching his desire June was undoing the small hooks holding the front of her blouse closed, quickly followed by undoing the clip holding her bra together.

Both were looking at each other in wonderment and unashamed passion, feeling the yearning in the other. Dennis felt his mouth had gone dry, his hands were trembling as he lowered his jeans as he watched June removing her blouse and bra, his eyes mesmerised by the white flesh.

She melted into his arms. She felt his strength sending new pleasant feelings all the way through her spine. He held her for a moment before kissing her gently on the neck and down across her chest.

The feeling of anticipation and being wanted swept through her and she could feel her breasts tightening. She had never had feelings like it before, in all her married life. She had never wanted her husband as much as she wanted this man, who she had only met a few hours ago.

She felt and wanted more to hold him and watch the pleasure on his face at what she was doing. The lust for him was rising and the need was now. She pulled away from him and lowered her skirt and petticoats, picking them up slowly, savouring the moment as she felt Dennis's eyes following her every move. Now only wearing brief underwear and stockings she laid down on the bed.

He knelt beside her, kissing her, stroking and teasing her nipples. She laid very still taking pleasure in the sensation and his gentleness.

She could sense and could see he was very excited. strengthening her desire and yet also being a little frightened. He lay down beside her stroking a leg and inner thigh. It was too much for June, she wanted him, and pulling Dennis towards her they kissed deeply.

He lay beside her for a moment wide eyed and taking deep breaths while admiring her. She lay down on her back her whole body afire with wanting him, she whispered in a husky voice "Now Dennis, please!" She pulled him on top of her.

She started to scream with pleasure. The world vanished as she absorbed him. His urgency came to an end and they lay in each other's arms exploring their naked bodies making love again with less urgency and a deeper satisfaction.

June felt alive and unbelievably happy, all jealousy gone and yet knowing her marriage would not be the same again. They had very little sleep each passionately aware of the others need and continued exploring each other until the early hours.

Declan O'Donnell

Dressed smartly in evening suits Tony and Declan met once more at The Black Rose. They were sitting at a corner table and after enjoying their meal they were talking in low terms.

"Has it been decided to go with my suggestion?" It was Tony asking the question as he played with the stem of his wine glass.

"Have you made any progress with finding the kegs or barrels?" He was looking around him as if the conversation had no importance.

"Yes, they are not too difficult to obtain, they can be modified down at the house in Croydon." He paused and looked around him before continuing. "One of our people inspected the cellars and we know exactly where to plant the device, it will need to be set off by someone inside the building. As I understand any other way may not activate it"

Declan was nodding his head "Did you see the sign when we came in to say there is a Party Night here in a few weeks time. I've been before, it is an evening when the place is very busy and normally the Army is here, and it is none other than the Parachute Regiment. We also have someone lined up who has a particular hate for them."

"Do I know them?" the other shook his head "I don't think so – but enough said I think we should leave." He waved over to the waiter and asked him for the bill.

June

Sunday morning dawned bright and warm. June woke to the singing of the birds and the feeling of being in a strange room. The sound of breathing coming from the other side of the bed brought her wide awake.

The previous evening came flooding back to her, and now that the drink had worn off, the activities of the previous hours took on a new dimension and the old inhibitions returned.

She could feel her nakedness under the sheets and embarrassment swept through her. She lay very still not daring to wake Dennis, and yet she knew sooner or later she would have to face him and the others.

How could she possibly lay in her husband's arms after this without the thought of the past evening coming into her head?

While she went over the events in her mind she felt a stirring in the bed. His hands crept round her and she could feel his hardness pressing into her. Once again she felt the pleasure of him and the gentle rhythm, and knew her embarrassment had gone.

Sometime later June realised he had gone back to sleep, sliding out from under the covers, she gathered her clothing and vanished into the bathroom.

Half an hour passed when June went through the living room and smiled at the screen still standing like a white square monument to the previous evenings activities. She was in the kitchen searching for the coffee things, when Kay came into the room a dressing gown wrapped around her, the prettiness and beauty of the previous evening a sad memory.

Sitting down on a stool at the breakfast bar she looked at her guest through bleary eyes. "Dennis is going to be disappointed he likes a hump in the morning?"

June looked at this woman she had barely met feeling embarrassed at the way she talked about sex, she said "Oh!" No other words would follow and yet she felt she should say something. Nodding her head, she added "about an hour ago he's now gone back to sleep."

"That's some guy you got there, he's so strong, I bet he gives you a lot of pleasure."

"Oh!" She repeated not knowing what else to say and thinking '*they are all sex mad in this house.*' She turned from the stove and gave a weak smile "Should we insist they get up for breakfast?"

"If you take it up to him you are liable to be his breakfast. He doesn't believe the arrangement has come to an end until you go home the following day."

She almost said 'oh' again however June managed to stop herself from repeating it and instead said "In that case, he had better get up for it."

"Are you talking about breakfast?"

"Yes, breakfast!" She was finding it difficult to understand all the innuendos which Kay seemed to revel in "Is Michael awake?"

"Just - I left him making his way to the bathroom. What time are you leaving?"

"After we have something to eat." She smiled at her new friend. "If that is okay?"

Kay nodded her head "That's okay. Have you enjoyed yourself – me, I have had a ball?"

"Quite an experience – yesterday I wanted to call it off."

"And now?" Kay was smiling which seemed to be a permanent feature.

Picking up the cup of coffee she said "When do we come back?" June had a wide grin on her face as the feeling of embarrassment was fading.

"If you are serious then we can work something out." There was movement from the living room with Michael appearing in the doorway.

"I would like that but only if we can all go to that superb restaurant again." She added as if any other activity was furthest from her mind. Michael looked at her in surprise. She just grinned back at him.

It was nearly midday when they finally got away. June had found the time going quickly in a relaxed atmosphere, the conversation easy as if the previous evening's enjoyment had not existed.

After breakfast the two women cleared away the table and departed into the kitchen whilst the two men walked in the garden.

Sometime later Michael and June drove away in silence both with their own thoughts. Finally, he broke the quietness between them "Was it what you expected?"

"No, I thought I would hate it, and yet I felt the opposite and adored it immensely." She turned her head and looked at him, a big grin on her face "In fact, I can't wait to get you in bed tonight."

Michael's mouth went dry – he glanced at her as he had never heard his wife speak like that before.

All of a sudden, he felt nervous, it was not what he had expected, and he could not help thinking that perhaps the evening had been a big mistake. "Oh, I didn't think you would go through with it."

"I was in two minds at first – now I feel different...liberated would be too grand a word, but I have the feeling things are not going to be the same."

"I don't know if I should feel flattered or not – in one breath you are saying you want me and then follow it up as if you have been bored with me, and I have not made you happy."

"I'm sorry, I did not mean it to sound as if I was not happy with you – but as I said I do feel different, although if and when we do it again it will not have the same remarkable excitement – nevertheless I am going to look forward to it."

Michael felt as if he was being sucked into a void, he had thought it would be a one off and now he felt he had started something he did not know how to stop. "Is there going to be a second time?" His voice sounded nervous and somewhere deep down there were stirrings he did not want.

"Why not?" she replied smiling at him then changing the subject she said as they passed a tall building "Isn't that the restaurant we met them in last night – that seems a long time ago."

The Black Rose

The Black Rose, with its extensive car park and numerous outbuildings, was a huge grand old structure which had been initially built by a wealthy business man two hundred years before, as his family home.

The original details to the ceilings and the plaster work had been retained, although now the ground floor, which had been a series of fine rooms for the former household had now been converted into two bars, a Public and a grander Saloon with a lounge to the side.

A little further on the original dance hall, which was a lot older than the house, had been retained and was used for private functions.

The outside of the building was still in its finery of design as when it was first built, with the exception of the added neon signs advertising a Restaurant and Casino.

The interior and been totally changed and appeared to have originated from the Edwardian period, with wooden panels and pillars, although looking real, in reality they were fibreglass reproductions.

Hanging red lamp shades with tassels, imitation velvet covered seating, potted plants and framed pictures completed the picture, which at the same time as being attractive gave the impression of being smoky and stuffy.

The Public Bar was totally different and very plain in comparison and was mainly used by the local community from the nearby housing estate.

The remainder of the premises was geared to supplying a first class service to the travellers on the main road between London and Guildford, which passed close by to the old house.

Behind the property and hidden by tall poplar trees lay a new industrial development, its individual designed complexes spread through a maze of roads – some making components for industry, others turning out consumer products.

During the lunch period, The Black Rose was the scene of many business deals as the manufacturers of the estate entertained past and new clients in the facilities offered by the licensee.

The car driven by Declan O'Donnell accompanied by another Irish friend Lewis, pulled up outside the old mansion only to find the car park was nearly full. Declan sometimes known as Ginger, had difficulty in parking the big Mercedes saloon. Without saying a great deal, they walked over to the main entrance.

Inside the restaurant was busy, which was not unusual for any day of the week. The two new arrivals stood at the crowded bar having first indicated to the waiter they wanted to eat. While they waited for the menu, Declan ordered drinks and carried on the conversation that they had been having in the car, as if the venue had not changed.

A little way along the bar stood a twin flash of khaki, complete with polished Sam Brown Belts over smartly pressed uniforms. The two officers, with paratrooper insignia, were in a jolly mood, both holding glasses, one a scotch the other a gin and tonic with a portion of sliced lemon fitted to the rim.

It was not unusual for the Army to be at the bar, however normally they were in civilian clothes. Today was different as they had come straight from the parade rehearsal for recruits who had passed their training at the barracks a few miles away. On the following day, when the actual parade took place in front of the Commanding Officer, then dinner would be served in the Officers mess using the Regimental silver.

Traditionally on rehearsal day the officers came down to The Black Rose for a more informal meal and the two standing at the bar were waiting for the others to join them.

Terry Parks, the head waiter, who was the longest serving member of staff, was taking an order from two clients who had been waiting for a while, and his experience told him they were getting impatient.

He was not worried about the Army for he knew they would stand at the bar for some time before wishing to order. As he wrote out the slip which would be passed to the kitchen, he was aware that it was building up to be a very busy lunchtime. No problem to him, he liked being active and if it got a bit hectic then so what?

As he passed the two men in uniform, one of them caught his eye. Stopping he asked them if they were ready to order.

"Not yet, Terry – but if you could make sure there is a table available in say about half an hour."

"Of course, no problem - how many will there be?"

"The usual crowd Terry, about ten, I'm not sure if the Major is coming." He said it as if the waiter should know of a reason why he would not be.

As they turned to the bar to resume their drinks Terry interrupted them "By the way did you know the Governor and his wife are leaving?"

"No, when are they going?" They both had a look of total surprise on their faces.

"Two or three weeks time, in the evening there is going to be a bit of a party, why don't you lot come down for it?"

"I say, that is not a bad idea, the lads like a party we could also have a meal at the same time and make a proper 'do' of it".

The Captain of the two spoke for the first time "I'm not certain if we could all fit in with that arrangement."

The lieutenant leaning against the bar looked a little surprised at his companion "Why not Ian?"

"Other commitments and it would not do to have a thick head the following day."

"You are making excuses and thinking of that bird you are having an affair with, and you can't bear to leave her alone for one evening." He had spoken softly so the words could not be overheard.

Terry Parks felt embarrassed as he had heard the remarks and departed without saying another word, leaving the two officers to carry on their conversation.

The officer, with two pips on his shoulder, was saying, "You know it would be different, and perhaps the ladies could join us or at least meet them afterwards?"

The Captain, with a smile on his face and picking up his drink at the same time, said "I see enough of you lot all day – without spending an evening at the weekend with you as well. Anyway we will see what the others have got to say?"

In the far corner sitting on identical wooden chairs with red padded seats, were Declan and Lewis the two Irish men leaning on a small round table where they had just had a brief lunch.

Although they had originally planned to be dressed more smartly on the day, thinking it would be in the evening but as it was lunch time they had not bothered. They stood out from the rest of the customers, their casual tee shirts and jeans were so diverse and poles apart from the other clientele – most of whom were dressed in jackets and ties.

Terry Parks, when he had first seen them enter his domain, had pulled a face and was tempted to inform them to go into the Public Bar. On the other hand, he had been told by Burt, on previous occasions, that it was none of his business what people wore and where they sat. He mentally shrugged his shoulders and turned away determined not to look at them.

A few minutes later he could not resist turning his head to see them and noticed they were in deep conversation leaning across the table, the person speaking had his hand in front of his mouth.

"Well Declan, there must be a reason for meeting here – do I sense it has got something to do with the coming operation?"

Declan was smiling and nodding his head "Yes, I came here recently for the second time with Tony and we are now ready to move forward with the planning. Don't say anymore, I will give you details when we are outside. So, drink up and we will be on our way."

Terry Parks was pleased to see them get up from the table and make their way to the door, however he was wondering what one of them found so interesting the way he was looking around.

The pair got into their car and looked at the building from where it was parked. Declan was speaking "I wanted to see again the chosen site for myself. Now what I understand is where we were sitting was immediately above the cellars, and that is where the explosives will be planted."

"How do I achieve that?" the other was shaking his head saying "you don't have to, that will be the responsibility of others. What you need to do is to make yourself known by frequent visits with the girl and when the time is right press the button, which will be hidden in the girls' handbag."

"Well Declan what's this Frances like – is she a pretty girl ... not too pretty we don't want her standing out?"

"She is just perfect for what we need and has a lasting grudge against the English." He paused and looking at The Black Rose. "I'm was not too happy with that waiter who kept looking our way – anyway you asked me if she was pretty – you wouldn't throw her out of bed."

"As I am going to be working with her when do I get to meet her?"

"All in good time. I will need to know she can carry out the work so she will need training and then you can spend some time together."

He turned and looked at him seriously "Now, understand what I am saying ... keep your sexual urges in check and your sadistic attitude, there is a job to be done and it would not look right if she arrives at the venue covered in bruises."

He looked at his companion sternly "You do understand me Lewis – don't you?" the other was nodding his head and looking out of the side window.

Declan continued "When the time comes, I want the two of you to be able to act naturally as one, if you hurt her she won't be relaxed and you will stand out and people will be suspicious.

I have said enough, we had better get out of here." He started the car and they drove away, he said "It is important that it is she who presses the buttons, you do understand that?" The other nodded his head.

June

June Whitehead looked through the kitchen window, at the darkening sky as she fumbled in the suds gathered on the top of the washing up water. Taking out the final spoon and putting it with the other items on the draining board of the stainless steel sink unit, her mind was on other things than the washing up or the rain that swept the garden.

She was thinking of a night of love in a stranger's bed. As she thought about it butterflies fluttered in her stomach and tingles ran through her as she remembered the details still vividly impressed on her mind.

Pulling the plug from the bottom of the sink she automatically rinsed the washing up water away leaving the unit tidy. As she reached for a towel to dry her hands, the telephone startled her as it was demanding attention with its shrill ringing.

Dropping the towel back on its hook she made her way into the hall to answer it, mildly wondering who it could be.

Three miles away, the person who was in a lustful mood had been thinking of her.

Despite the rain and the awful weather, he left the warmth of his car and approached a phone box, only to see the receiver hanging by its lead and the coin box broken open. Realising it was of no use as he looked for another, only for the same result.

With the thought of her soft warm body he was determined to call her and finally he found a call box which was in working order and not vandalised.

He stood with the earpiece clamped to his ear listening to the burr-burr of the ringing tone; the wind was blowing drops of rain onto him through one of the broken panes of glass that adorned the call box.

He heard the connection being made and recognised her voice as she repeated the telephone number by way of an answer – he thought she sounded nervous.

He took a deep breath "Hello, is that you June?"

"Yes, who's that?" She had no need to ask as she already knew by recognising the soft strong voice. The butterflies had started again as she waited for him to reply.

"Hi June! Dennis – remember me. I'm not far away and I thought I might pop round for a cup of coffee - that is, of course, if you care to invite me?" It was said in such a way that assumed she would say 'yes'.

"Well, I had planned to go out." She lied, her heart racing, part of her not wanting to get involved. However, she knew she would be.

"In that case I won't be able to stay long. I'll make a deal with you, a cup of coffee in exchange for a trip to wherever you wish to go?"

"How do you know I haven't already got a lift?" she could feel herself wanting to see him as the excitement of a clandestine meeting swept through her.

"I don't. I'm just guessing. You told me you didn't drive – you remember, I offered when we last met, to teach you. Who knows this could be your first lesson?"

"Of course!" she went silent. Part of her wanting to say yes, the other part telling her she didn't want anything to do with him. He was a threat to her tidy lifestyle and she could not see any good coming from the involvement.

She realised she was taking a long time to answer. The thought of those stolen hours, in that strange bedroom, flooded through her thoughts, and the practicality of her way of life went out of her mind. She was flattered that he wanted to see her again and she was saying "How long will you be?" those funny little sexual feelings started to chase through her and yet in some way she was disappointed in herself for agreeing to meet him.

"I thought for a moment you had left me – and it is so cold and draughty in this phone box." He was looking at a traffic warden walking towards his car. "June, I have got to go there is a traffic warden interested in my car, I'll see you shortly."

She was not certain but thought he had rung off but then she heard him breathing "Do you know the way to our house?"

"I think so I have looked it up on a road map – I must go, I'll be there in about ten or fifteen minutes."

June looked in the mirror above the telephone table and saw her hair was in a mess, that annoying strand, which would insist on falling over her eye. She brushed it away while she looked around the room to see if everything was in its place.

A short time later she was in her bedroom throwing off her housework clothing and looking in the wardrobe for something that would suit the occasion. Settling on jeans, with no bra, and a shirt tugged into them, she sat at the dressing table adjusting her make-up and confident the house was acceptable to visitors.

She was dabbing perfume behind her ears when June heard the car, long before the door chimes, creating a nervous reaction and a change of mind was racing through her – *'she didn't have to answer the door and after a short while he would go away.'*

She pushed the thought out of her psyche and brushing that curl away from her face again. She was in no hurry, teasing him and keeping him waiting in the rain gave her a certain amount of satisfaction, and slowly made her way down the stairs. On reaching the door she turned the latch, her heart leapt as she saw him, pushing the lock of hair to one side, she smiled and opened the door wide.

"My, you look nice" Dennis was standing on the step, windswept with a grin on his face and a bottle of vodka in his hand, and his eyes sweeping over her.

"Thank you" she couldn't help smiling, adding "come in out of the cold." admiring his well-groomed attire and his broad shoulders. She showed him into the living room thinking to herself *'did I really lay in his arms and let him do all those things to me.'*

He held the bottle up as if it was a trophy and offered it to her "I thought perhaps a small drink would go down better than coffee." When she did not take it he put it down on the glass top coffee table in front of the 'L' shape dark brown leather settee, at the same time taking off his outdoor coat.

"Oh! I don't usually drink during the day, and I'm not sure I should start...anyway what would Michael say if he found out I had been drinking, he would wonder what I had been up to."

He thought *'why did she have to mention her husband and spoil the atmosphere between them'* "Actually it is for that reason I brought vodka they tell me that the smell of alcohol does not stay on the breath." He knew by the tone of her voice she was going to join him in a glass and asked, "have you got any tonic to go with it?"

She had gone over to the drink's cabinet saying "Somewhere at the back of the shelf here I should find a bottle, it is not a thing we drink regularly." June brought out a bottle of the clear liquid "And I guess there will be some ice in the fridge, sit down while I get it."

June made her way into the kitchen her thoughts in a whirl; she was flattered, she could not remember the last time a man had taken such a step as to call on her at home, in fact it had not happened before. She knew only too well what he wanted, but the drink he had brought had caught her off guard and if she did not call a halt to it now it could get out of hand.

She returned to the living room holding the ice tray on a plate saying "Well, one quick drink and then back to work." She looked into his face and their eyes met, she stood for a moment not knowing what to do as the need for him swept through her.

"Look...Dennis..." her voice trailed away. The memory of unbuttoning his shirt and pushing it back across his shoulders flooded through her.

Holding two glasses, one in each hand, which he had retrieved from a cabinet while she was in the kitchen. He was still smiling at her and asking "Yes?"

"I was just thinking it was great fun last week. But..."

"But what? Surely a little drink and a chat won't do any harm." He sat down "I got the glasses from the cabinet over there." He made a gesture in the direction of where the glasses were kept. "Are they the right ones?" His eyes were locked into hers.

June did not have the strength to refuse and anyway, she was not certain if she wanted to '*didn't I get the tonic and the ice,'* "Just a small one I don't want to be rolling around when Michael gets home." He thought *'there she goes again mentioning Michael'*

He stood up and was holding out two cut glass tumblers and using her fingers she put a piece of ice into each one. Looking into his face she said "I'll let you pour – not too much mind." The need of the drink was slipping away as she could see he was aroused, and June felt the longing for him cursing through her.

She was too captivated by him and dismissed the earlier thoughts of trying to bring the afternoon to an early close.

Glancing at the clock she knew she had plenty of time. Trembling with the thought of the next hour or so she watched as he skillfully poured the liquid into the glasses.

With a strong lovely feeling chasing through her she acknowledged the salute he gave with the glass and anticipated what would happen next.

He took the glass from her hand and she remembered that is what he had done in the bedroom, she slipped into his arms and they came together in a deep kiss. June was past caring, and she pushed him backwards and the settee got in the way of his legs and he sat down.

He watched with a dry mouth and shaking hands as June slowly undone the shirt she was wearing displaying her bare breasts, pleased with herself for not wearing a bra.

She slowly got down on her knees in front of him and leaning over him started to remove the belt holding his jeans in place.

He froze, looking at her beautiful form as she sat back on her haunches displaying her wonderful bare torso, was she really going to do what he thought she was.

Looking up at him with a smile on her face, she leant forward again rubbing both hands up his legs and across his thigh. Reaching for his zip she started to lower it slowly with only one thought in mind, and that was to pleasure this new love.

The Black Rose

The Public Bar was crowded and the early evening regulars at The Black Rose were making plans for the going away presentation for the Landlord and his wife some of whom they had known for twenty or more years.

To one side of the long wide area were two 'one armed bandits' also known as 'fruit machines' each had a person putting coins in a slot after which, pulling the long handle to the side towards them with a loud clonk, this made a set of three wheels, with pictures of fruit on them spinning. There was an occasional moan when the lines of images were not equal.

Further down the room with a variety of different coloured lights flashing, the juke box was playing a latest hit tune, and someone who was knowledgeable about the machine, had reached up behind it to the controls, which altered the sound, and turned the volume up.

Scattered around the room were tables and chairs some with spilt beer to their tops but most of those present were standing at the bar.

The cluster of people, in the main were all men, mostly self employed tradesmen, and their customary attendance at the bar was to relax from a hard day's work. Although each recognized most of those in attendance, it was not by name, more from their appearance.

The group had gathered there on this occasion to discuss buying s present for the very popular landlord and his wife who were leaving the pub in a few weeks' time and being replaced by another.

Amongst a group leaning against the bar, one of whom spoke. "The problem as I see it is how are we going to organize the whole thing without them knowing?" The speaker, who was leaning with his back to the bar, had one hand in his pocket

Almost in a whisper came a stern reply "Well, we could all speak a little bit quieter." as if the speaker did not want anyone to hear.

"Nobody can hear us." Said a balding man, in his early forties, wearing overalls with a peaked cap tucked into a pocket.

"If you ask me, we have been talking about it for so long, it would be better to forget the whole thing, because at this rate we will never come to a decision." The speaker, up to that moment had not said a word, he seemed to have been quite content sitting on the edge of the circle reading a newspaper.

"The amount of interest you have shown in the subject so far as been nothing but negative. Negative thoughts that is all we get from you - that's real bad man." The speaker was the youngest of the group wearing a bright tee shirt with matching trainers, who was a swimming teacher at the local baths run by the Council.

"Well, why don't you come up with something constructive?" It was the man with the paper talking.

"What do you mean...?" The youngest was looking hurt he did not like criticism and felt embarrassed.

At that moment there was a shout from one of the players on the fruit machine, and the loud clatter of coins falling, as he had won the five pound jackpot of sixpenny pieces. A cheer went up around the room and someone shouted 'It's your round.'

The first speaker with one hand in his pocket intruded the noise "Now come on fellows that's enough of that. Let's get down to some sensible decisions."

Looking around the group for support, some were nodding their heads, but saying nothing. He continued "Here's an idea, why don't we decide on a treasurer and then the profits from the Saturday evening darts match and the raffle, instead of going to the darts team funds, be used for some form of gift. We could get the wives to go out shopping the week before they leave."

"What about the Darts Team money – why should they suffer?" Ron, up to that moment had not appeared to be listening to the conversation and had been taking long gulps from the pint of dark ale, wiping his mouth with his sleeve after each swallow. He suddenly had taken a lot of notice at the mention of darts as he was one of the team's active members.

"Well the team has plenty of funds at the moment- when we are selling the tickets, we could explain what the money is for, and perhaps get better support."

"I thought this was going to be a secret – if we tell the whole pub, they will get to know in no time at all." It was the man with the newspaper talking.

"There you go again with those negative waves – why don't you..." somebody told him to shut up.

"Will you two stop fighting?" The first voice said sharply "Alright, I agree, perhaps it is not a good idea to tell the whole world. So what we could say the funds are needed for a special occasion..."

He was cut short by a small wily man who had been sitting listening with interest "That would be dishonest."

"No, not really, the funds would be for a special purpose." Replied the first speaker.

"Yeah – but suppose the people buying the tickets don't like the Governor?" As the Landlord was sometimes affectionately called.

"Well they would hardly be drinking in here would they?" Asked a cockney voice who had been fiddling with his pipe and had stopped trying to light it to pass the remark, continuing with his ritual after he had spoken as if he had not interrupted the process.

The second voice spoke while everyone was still completing the logic of the last answer. "I think we should stop all this bickering and get down to some detail. I don't even know when they are supposed to be going."

The pipe moved between the wearers teeth "Blimey, mate wake up - where you been it has been the talk of the bar for weeks?"

Newspaper man was turning a page and joined in "Easter week, I thought everyone knew."

"My God some people go around with their ears closed." Remarked tee shirt

"You don't have to be offensive." Replied the second speaker.

"I still think it is dishonest." Added the short one "In fact I could not agree to such..."

"You are not being asked to agree, just listen while we positive souls make a decision..." Tee shirt was interrupted as if he had not been speaking.

"We must get on with it and make some sort of plan – the governor and his missus will be down in a minute to run the bar for the evening..."

"It's Wednesday – it will be the missus." Said the short one.

"Does it really matter which one it is?" Said newspaper who had stopped reading.

"Of course it doesn't matter, but we have got to come to some decision before they arrive otherwise, if it is supposed to be a surprise we will not be able to talk about it in front of them."

"Here, here." Said another voice and then "How are we going to make the presentation – if all these people have been paying into a fund, they will want to know what was bought."

Tee shirt looked up from making faces with his finger out of the spilled beer on the bar top "Man, what are you talking about – we get together one evening just before they go, about ten o'clock would be a good time."

"Why?" the pipe moved up and down in the speaker's mouth.

"What do you mean 'why?' that is when everybody is a bit merry, we can have a roll on the drums – make the presentation, have a few of the lads from the press here to take some pictures – give him a round of 'for he's a jolly good fellow,' and half a dozen of us put him on our shoulders and march him around the bar."

Nobody said anything although someone murmured 'he's a big guy.'

Tee shirt asks "Does anyone know where their daughter lives I think she should be here?" At that moment the jukebox ran out of money and a murmur went around the group asking who's turn it was to put more money into the machine.

One of the group went over to start the music again, while Ron said he knew she worked in a bank in the High Street and offered to call in and tell her when all the details were agreed.

"Right!" the first speaker looked around the group "are we all agreed we should have a treasurer and I think he should be responsible for obtaining the going away present?"

There were nods around the group, nobody was showing too much enthusiasm in case they got saddled with the job. As the speaker continued there were coughs and fidgeting around the table "Well – the next question is who is it going to be?"

After further discussion in which no one noticed the Missus coming into the bar, it was decided that Ron should hold the honorary post as he was already treasurer of the darts team. He was showing reluctance at accepting the responsibility but was secretly pleased as it was a kind of endorsement for the work he did for the dart team.

Irene realizing what was going on, although she was curious, decided to hide by serving in the other bar until they had finished, leaving the serving in the public bar to one of the part time staff

Declan O'Donnell

Declan O'Donnell sometimes known as 'Ginger' slid his large black car to a stop in Kilburn High Street outside a café which was squeezed in between other shops. He sat for a moment with the engine running and watched through the window as Tony drained his cup and left the premises and got into the car next to him.

The big vehicle slid away from the curb with Declan checking his mirrors to see if they were being followed. Satisfied they were not, he said "We have brought the girl over from Ireland." He glanced at his passenger to see if he was listening.

The other did not reply immediately expecting something further, "What do you want me to do?"

"Currently she is staying at a house in North London." He was still checking to see if they were being followed.

"Not that filthy place just off the Holloway road, she must be at her wits end with that somber Irish woman and the permanent dirty overall?"

"Yes, I know what you mean I had the misfortune of staying there, just once and overnight, something I would not want to do again." He looked at his passenger with one of his rare smiles. "She has been there a few days now and we think it is time she moved as we are getting close to the operation."

"What are you asking me to do?"

"Go round there and take her out a few times, we want you to buy her some clothes so she will feel good in herself – you know what I mean, the latest fashion, we do not want her looking out of place. The police are getting inquisitive since the last two attacks we have made, so we need her looking right."

"Okay, that will be a pleasure doing that, then what?" He looked at the other with an inquisitive look on his face.

"The main thing is not to tell her anything, at the moment she must not know what we are planning. Next Monday, those tea rooms you were in, just now when I picked you up, take her there where you will introduce her to Lewis, after that my friend you are going back to Ireland."

He looked at Declan with surprise "Why would I want to do that?"

"Mainly for your own protection - for you see we do not know if she has been recognized by the Police, if they have, then they will have a link to you. So you will pass her over to Lewis and leave the country. You do understand, don't you?" The other nodded his head.

June & Michael

June was upstairs having just got rid of Dennis by gently pushing him out of the door, as he had been reluctant to go.

She was changing back into clothing she normally wore when working around the house, when she heard a car pull up outside.

At first she thought it was her visitor returning and then realized it sounded more like Michael's car. She went into the bathroom to finish off what she was doing.

She heard him call out as he came through the front door, and shouted back telling him where she was, adding "You are home early?"

"There is some dispute at the works which did not seem to be resolved today. As we had nothing to do, we called it a day – shall I put the kettle on?"

June thanked her lucky stars that Michael had not come home even earlier.

She wondered what he would have said or done if he had found Dennis here. Then she thought to hell with him, it was he who had started the arrangement, she had been very happy before he had suggested, and made the agreement with Dennis and Kay.

Perhaps for all she knew he had been seeing someone on the side and it had been going on for some time.

As she got herself changed and tidied her hair, she was developing the thought, but dismissed it as soon as it started convinced, she would have noticed something.

Anyway, his job as a warehouse manager kept him busy and when he was not working, he was at home. But she could not help wondering how many other times the employees of the firm had been on strike, and instead of coming home, going somewhere he should not have done.

A lot later, after the evening meal, they had settled down to watch their favorite programs on the television. She suddenly got up and poured them both a drink.

"This is unusual – what are we celebrating?"

Shrugging her shoulders "Nothing! I just thought it would make a change."

"That's nice – cheers." He raised his glass to her, and she responded.

PERCY W. CHATTEY

They both went back to looking at the small screen, but he could sense there was something troubling her. He looked at her "You are deep in thought tonight, what's bothering you?"

June turned and smiled at him "Not a lot."

"So this little thing that is bothering you, are you going to tell me about it?" his eyes had left the screen and he was looking at her.

"Nothing to tell really – how long is this strike going on for?" She had also taken her eyes away from the television and was looking into the glass of liquid.

"I don't know...I should imagine it will all be over tomorrow – why do you ask?"

"I just wondered if you will be going into work in the morning?" she had turned to face him.

"Of course!" He was looking at her with a questioning look on his face, feeling that she wanted to say something and was trying to find a way to say it.

"Michael..." Instead of continuing she took a sip of her drink.

He found it annoying and prompted her by saying "Yes?" He was starting to feel upset at her coyness *after all these years why couldn't she just come out with what she wanted to say?*'

Instead of replying she took another sip of her drink. "Well, what is it?" he said a little too sharply. Trying to guess what she was trying to say as she seemed to be unusually coy.

She took a deep breath and with exciting thoughts tinkling through and at the same time feeling totally embarrassed said "I was wondering if we could go and see that couple again?"

He almost dropped his drink in surprise "What! Do you mean that Dennis fellow and that insipid woman?"

"I don't remember you describing her like that after you had been with her, as I remember you said she was 'a right little raver' or something like that."

She was looking at him a smile tugging at the corners of her mouth. "Well that was different – and anyway, we agreed it would only be for the once." But he could not stop feeling excited at the thought of seeing Kay again.

"We did not agree that – it was what you suggested when you were trying to get me to agree to what you wanted." June smiled sweetly at him.

By now the television programme was of little interest to them and was only serving as an aid to help them through the occasional uncomfortable silences.

It was his turn to look into the vodka in his glass thinking *'I did not know we had vodka in the house.'*

is wife interrupted his thought. "Well wasn't that what you said she was? And as I remember you couldn't keep your hands off her by pulling her skirt up – what there was of it. "

"Perhaps, anyway you weren't being very reserved you couldn't take your eyes off him. What's come over you? You're like the cat that's been at the cream. Why this unexpected interest in this other guy?"

Suddenly he felt threatened and was wishing he had never suggested the idea originally. Whilst the thought of a second session was not without its excitement, he didn't want his wife suggesting it, it made him feel vulnerable as if he wasn't in control.

"No sudden interest, I thought you had enjoyed the evening, and I thought you would like to repeat the eah..."

"The eah...what?" He was looking at her a little sternly.

She slipped off the chair to kneel at his feet, sensing his nervousness, she wanted to be nearer to him. She started tracing small patterns on his thigh whilst she smiled up into his eyes.

"Eah... nothing Michael, I just wanted you to be happy, and I know you got pleasure from the evening, and I thought you would like to do it again, and that's why I'm suggesting it."

Gradually he had a feeling there was a lot more to the request of repeating the exchange of partners, and he was certain she had been seeing this Dennis "You haven't been up to anything have you?" His voice had gone a little hard.

"What do you mean?" She looked up at him with a hurt look on her face.

"Well, first you ask me if I'm going to work tomorrow..."

"How could you?" still on her knees, she sat up, she took her hands away and was glaring into his face showing she was hurt by what he was signifying.

"Don't do that; put your hand back I liked what you were doing. Anyway, I'm sorry for what I said I should not have suggested you had been doing anything. Can we start again?"

"Where do you want to start?" It was said with a teasing smile.

"You could put your hand back."

"You are only interested in one thing." She leant forward on to his knees.

He started to stroke her hair looking down at the swell of her breasts, "I was jealous of you."

"You never were, you never had time to be jealous, and anyway I don't think you have ever been jealous of me."

"Well, I may not show it, but it's true."

Having implied she was only thinking of him in arranging the meeting, she did not know how to keep him on the subject without making it look like it was she who really wanted to go back.

"What about when you were fondling that other woman, you did not once look at me, and you call that being jealous." The smile was still hovering around her lips.

"Don't split hairs and of course I could be thinking of you, anyway I think it's a bit soon to go back."

"I don't...anyway we could arrange something for the next few weeks."

"I do believe you want to see him again?"

"That's a silly statement, seeing that I brought the matter up."

He looked at her in almost disbelief, suddenly realising that she did want to. He was worried perhaps the whole thing had gone too far, perhaps she was falling in love with the guy.

"You really want to, don't you?" He said it with surprise on his face and a stirring in his groin as the thought spread through him.

She let her eyes drop "Yeh...shall I tell you why?" She said almost shyly.

"Please, I would like to know but I guess it is for the sex I suppose,"

She didn't raise her eyes, "It makes me feel so excited and good and very randy and it makes me want you more. especially when I'm with you after we have left them."

He didn't know what to say, "Do you?" He was looking at her puzzled, remembering how excited and demanding she had been the evening after they had left Dennis and Kay.

"It makes it all fresh, and new, and lovely." She had started to draw those invisible patterns on his leg again. "Darling, why don't you phone him now, go on its not too late." She added anticipating his look at the clock.

They sat in silence for a short while looking at each other. The conversation had made them both feeling very close to each other and June was also wondering if he would make the call.

He was letting exciting thoughts flow through him and the sheer joy of exploring Kay's wonderful body again. He slowly rose from the chair, although he was now certain there was more to it than she had said.

He went into the hallway of the house where the telephone receiver was. She could hear voices coming from just outside the room with the occasional laughter. Eventually she heard the telephone going 'ting' as he replaced the receiver. June was sipping her drink and smiling up at him as he came into the room.

PERCY W. CHATTEY

"They are all for it. We have arranged to meet next week, evidently it is Party Night at that restaurant we went to, and they are going to book the tickets."

They were looking at each other, their eyes locked together pushing previous thoughts away. She was smiling "Excited?" He nodded his head - going over to the television he turned it off.

Frances

Frances, who had been told to stay in the house, was not very happy as almost a week had gone past since her arrival in London. Her inability to leave the property was boring as there was only the television to watch, if not that then listening to the landlady moaning about prices or any other negative subject that came into her head.

Tony, who she understood was the local coordinate for the organisation, had visited her a few times during the week. Whilst his presence was some relief from the day to day routine, she had the distinct impression he had not come to talk about the event they had asked of her, when she had been ordered to go to the Capital city, but a desire to be a lot closer to her.

One day to her surprise he arrived and announced they were going shopping. Her heart lifted at the thought of being able to get out of this house.

Frances was rendered speechless when he told her they were going to buy her a new wardrobe of clothes. Feeling as if she had been insulted, for her thoughts were that she was always smartly dressed, nevertheless, the thought of having something different pleased her.

After the excitement of the shopping trip she returned to the old routine, but her spirits were lifted when he explained to her it was not too long now before she would be moving on.

Frances had awoken late, as was becoming her habit, to find it was still raining outside as it had been for some time, with a strong wind blowing. She felt even more depressed than she had all week.

Turning over and looking at her wristwatch, which was balanced on its side on the bedside table, she decided it was time to get up.

Today should be different as Tony was coming to collect her to meet another person, and they were going to start planning the operation. She wondered what nature it would take.

Putting all those thoughts out of her mind, she put on a dressing gown and going out into the cold dingy passage along to the scruffy bathroom, with its peeling paint, stained bath and smell of damp.

The ancient water heater balancing on a bracket above the tub spurted water which was trying to be hot but only managed a tepid flow. She shivered as she dropped her wrap to the floor and stepped into the barely warm water.

Her thoughts went back to happier times when, with her sister, they would play together and the comforting reassurance - looking at someone and seeing your own face and thoughts mirrored there. Frances felt the tears welling up in her eyes, she busied herself washing, pushing the hurtful pictures from her mind.

When Tony arrived, the girl was dressed and waiting, her long coat draped around her shoulders keeping her warm from the draughts that swept through the old neglected building.

He entered what was called the front room, not only because it was in the front of the house, but because it boasted two tatty easy chairs with a matching sofa, also a sparkling rented television, which with its newness looked out of place in its surroundings. Tony asked the obvious, "You ready?"

By way of an answer Frances, got up from where she had been sitting and moved towards the door, asking, "Where are we going?" His only reply was "Never you mind, lass, all in good time."

The journey was conducted most of the way in silence, Tony constantly looking about him, as if he was expecting to meet someone he knew. The girl also noticed that he was slightly nervous. When she asked what the problem was, she was quickly told to shut up.

After two changes of buses they arrived at a small cafe that was pressed between a sweet shop and large furniture store in Kilburn High Road. Despite the narrow entrance, inside it opened out with rows of chrome tube tables and chairs with blue padded seats and Formica tops. 'They bought two coffees from the bar that run down the right hand side.

Frances had noticed a fellow with dark curly hair sitting at a table towards the rear, he had looked up expectantly when they had walked through the door.

She was not surprised when they walked towards his table.

"What kept you, Tony?" His eyes were sweeping over Frances she pulled the coat around her as if for protection.

"Bloody buses...this is Frances." Nodding his head in the direction of the girl.

Lewis had already eyed her up as they had walked towards the table, and as he continued to speak to Tony he did not take his eyes off her, liking what he saw. "Well start out twenty minutes earlier next time, then you won't leave me sitting here wasting my time." Glancing at his colleague he added, "Come on Tony, aren't you going to introduce us?"

"I just did!" However, he repeated himself "This is Frances." Lewis looked at the girl who had now taken off her coat and was shaking the water from it before laying it across an empty chair, "That's Lewis, and he is going to look after you from now on" Tony completed the introduction.

She did not reply, just nodding her head across the table before sitting down feeling a bit uncomfortable because of his staring.

Before Lewis started speaking, he looked about him making certain that he could not be overheard, "You know what you are over here for, don't you?"

"Not exactly, only to get back at the English pigs." She glared at him as if he was some sort of moron.

"Whilst you are here it would be better if you kept your thoughts to yourself. It won't be for a few weeks yet, but you will have the opportunity to make a blow for the cause." As he spoke, she noticed that he hardly had any accent, what he did have was overshadowed by a strong London twang.

"What have you told her Tony?" Lewis glared at him daring him to say something.

"Nothing, just kept her company for a few, evenings."

"Yeah I bet you have!" Turning back to Frances he thought for a moment before speaking "Now look darling, this is what we are going to do, we won't go into the details of the operation, not yet anyway. You and I are going to get real friendly and be seen together at certain places, so people get used to us like, do you understand?"

She was looking bored as she gazed around her, nodding her head as she did so.

"Good. When we leave here you will be moving out of that fleapit and into a safe house the other side of London. Mind you, I'm not saying it's not safe where you are now but laughing boy here has been a little bit too clever and we think the Old Bill could be on to him."

She turned her head and looked at him with a surprised look on her face "'Old Bill??" she asked.

"Yeah darling, you know cops, police, pigs or whatever you want to call them"

"What's going to happen to him, will he go back to Ireland?"

"Never you mind! He'll lay low for a little while and then we will see. It is not good to know everything, and he will have had his own instructions, but it may be better if he went home for some time. But the point is, if they are on to him, they could have followed him and already know about the house where you are now, do you see?"

She nodded her head, her eyes glaring at him "I'm not stupid - what's happened, how have they got to know him?" she was thinking of her own position if they knew him then they would know her.

"You don't have to worry about it darling, as I just said it doesn't pay to know too much."

"Stop calling me darling!" She said sharply as she glared at him. "If they are on to him, I have a right and a need to know why!"

He could have told the girl, that on a night the previous weekend Tony, and two others, had learned where some explosives were stored, and without any planning they had decided to break into the building only to walk into a security guard who had got a good look at him. "Yes, you are right Frances - but now you know the ins and outs of why are not important."

"Tony, I think you have been told to go to ground and stay put until somebody gets in touch with you, anyway that has nothing to do with me. I'll take Frances home, and make the necessary arrangements for her to move. That way you will be out of it, until we get orders for what you should do."

"Oh, I am leaving this afternoon to catch the overnight boat back home."

Lewis looked at Tony with anger in his eyes "You know better than to talk of your movements, now get out and no doubt others will be in touch with you."

Frances spoke in a soft voice, "So I will not be going back to that house – I hope, wherever it is, it is better than that flea pit or I am leaving to go back to Euston Station and find a train that will take me home."

Lewis looked from one to the other "Okay Tony, I think it is time you vanished." They both watched as he left the coffee shop, pulling his collar up against the weather as he walked out of their sight.

"Now that he has left, I can tell you a little of what is going to happen...not too much, enough so that you know what we are planning. But first you will like your new home ... I think you will like it a lot!"

"Why didn't you say it in front of Tony ... is he such a real problem?"

"For the reasons I mentioned. We think he has been recognised" He waved his hand as to say enough is enough

"Don't you trust him?" He looked at her a little exasperated.

"If he gets arrested, it's not a matter of trust." She looked at him in surprise "What do you mean?"

It was his turn to look surprised "Will you stop asking silly questions, and listen...?" At that moment the meal they had ordered was called from the counter, he slipped from behind the table to go and fetch it.

Frances sat in silence and watched this person she was to work with feeling a numbness creeping through her as she realised the moment of truth was to hand. All the years of waiting – waiting to revenge the death of her father and her much loved sister and now not too long to wait and it would be hers.

And yet somewhere in her heart it was not what she really wanted. She glanced around the other tables, looking at the customers sitting, eating and talking –

some laughing. She could not remember the last time she had laughed. Perhaps, after she had taken the revenge she so craved on the English, some of the hurt would leave her and she would be able to laugh again and start a new life.

"You were deep in thought?" She looked up and felt the dislike she had first had for him resurface. She shrugged her shoulders and ignored the question. Taking the food out of his hands, unwrapping the knife and fork from the thin paper serviette, she started to eat.

"My God, you are a cold one. What makes you tick?"

She looked up at him with a frosty look, her memory flashing back to the day she held her sister in her arms watching her life ebb away, superimposed over a picture of her father falling dead across an already dead neighbour.

"Why don't you tell me more about what I am expected to do?"

"There's not a great deal to tell really, well not at this stage...that is." He paused and looked around him while he took a mouthful of food. "You will remember the day your father died?"

"How the hell could I forget a thing like that?" she said sharply.

"I don't know the details, you could tell me sometime...the officer in charge that day, is now with a training unit near Woking." He had taken another mouthful of food, she had put her knife and fork down looking at him intently.

"Every so often they have a celebration dinner in a local restaurant - which is really a pub."

"Where do I come in?" she looked at him in fascination.

"We need someone to plant the timing device." With wide eyes she looked at him nodding her head slightly. "How?" She almost whispered.

"All in good time. That is what you are here for. The point is - will you do it?"

"You bet I will. How long have I got to wait?" She could feel the excitement travelling through her as she stared at him looking and waiting for more information.

"Not too many weeks. Before then we will go through the details in greater depth. It's really very simple what you have to do, and I'll be about just in case."

"No need. Whatever needs doing, I'll do it with pleasure and a lot of satisfaction."

"Finish your meal and after I'll take you to some new lodgings. Tomorrow night we will go to the target, have something to eat and act natural."

She nodded her head. He had expected her to say something and when she didn't, he continued "We will keep going there for a little while until it is time to act and by then people will be used to seeing us, and what needs to be done will be that much easier."

The Women's Institute

Not very far from the Police Station in Guildford, and just off the main road in a side turning, and standing proudly on a corner between two roads, was an elderly wooden Scouts Hall.

It was originally given to the council by a wealthy benefactor and initially stood in three acres of grounds, with sports facilities, which had sadly been sold off, and was now the site of a small housing estate, built thirty years previously surrounding the Scouts facility.

The interior of this fine-looking structure demonstrated the skills of the carpenters who had put it together ninety years previously, with its vaulted roof and timber flooring.

Not only did the Scouts and like minded bodies use the premises as their home, it was also the venue where the local branch of the Women's Institute had their meetings.

A group of women were sitting around on aged wooden chairs, which someone in the past had supplied cushions for, in a floral pattern, to soften the seats.

The heating in the hall was nonexistent and one of the members had brought in a small electric fire, most of the heat from which vanished up into the rafters.

A sub-committee of the local W.I., an assembly of five, were in a corner, grouped around the small heating device all wearing outdoor clothing, trying to keep warm in the cold hall.

Vivian Dowling, a small dark haired lady, who acted as the Secretary for the Institute, was leaning forward and speaking "As everyone here already knows, our Chair Person, Doris Gilding, has been awarded a long service medal for her charitable work over thirty years. We agreed at a previous meeting that it should be presented to her as a surprise, and I am certain she still does not know about it."

A few murmurs went around the group, most of whom were nodding their heads and stretching their hands out as near to the heater as possible.

The Secretary was also holding her hand out over the fire and then continued. "I have had discussions with the Mayor's Office, and they have confirmed that the Mayor would be very pleased to present the award."

One of the group asked "Have they indicated where that will be?"

Although Vivian was very aware of what the arrangements were, she nevertheless opened a file resting on her lap retrieved a sheet of paper. Proudly holding it so everyone could see the heading on the letter was from the Mayor's office, she said. "The Mayor, with others, is due at The Black Rose in a few weeks time to attend a function there and he says it would be the ideal time to make the presentation." She looked around the group and noticed they were all nodding their heads.

Vivian was smiling as she continued "I thought as it will be forty years since the founding of this group around that time, we would put it to Doris that we should attend the function to celebrate the Institute achievements – that way she will not get suspicious of why we want to go there."

Before the meeting broke up that evening the arrangement was made to book a table at The Black Rose for the coming party Night.

Frances & Lewis

The house that Frances had been moved to was in South London, it was semi-detached on the outskirts of Croydon.

The property was surrounded by a high well-orderedly cut privet hedge, which effectively kept prying eyes from the road being able to see very much beyond it.

The home lay back from the small close it was in, and even the path leading to the old asbestos garage, which was in a poor state, had high hedges to each side.

In contrast to the garage the hedges and the lawns to the front of the house had been beautifully maintained and were an excellent illustration as to the gardener's abilities.

On approaching the house, it became apparent it was clean with its paintwork in good order, neat curtains hanging inside at the windows. In the rear, a neat tended garden leading to woodland over a small fence, which was one of the reasons the house had been chosen, many years previously.

Its occupants were a couple in their mid thirties, who had always kept themselves to themselves and shunning friendship of any kind as visitors were discouraged, because the house had a secret which had to be protected.

Frances, when she had first arrived had been very pleased as it was the complete opposite to where she had been staying. She was given a large room at the rear of the house overlooking the well kept rear garden. The space was pleasantly furnished, which included a double bed, the cover of which matched the curtains.

It was a few days after she had been there that Lewis came to visit her in the afternoon. It was still raining, but for short breaks, it had not stopped for most of the time. Once in the front door he threw his wet raincoat over the stair banisters and walked straight up the stairs to find the girl, having been given a nod in that direction from the woman who had opened the door to him.

She was sitting at a small table staring out of the window, where she could see an equally tidy and neat lawn similar to the front one, followed by a well tended vegetable patch, before three single strands of wire that represented the bottom fence leading into the deep undergrowth of the trees.

She turned as the door was pushed open, "Oh, it's you?" no emotion showing on her face.

"Were you expecting someone else?"

A sad smile crossed her face as she answered, "Who else is there?" She turned to look out into the garden again.

"What are you looking at?" He had walked into the room and was standing behind her.

"There was a squirrel climbing that tree, it's vanished into the branches now...when are we going to get down to whatever we are supposed to be doing?" Her face did not move as she looked over her shoulder to ask the question.

"First we must teach you something about explosives, we wouldn't want you blowing yourself up, not a pretty thing like you." He was talking friendly.

"You can save that kind of talk for the other women in your life." She continued looking through to the garden, talking softly as if it did not matter.

"What's so different about you, perhaps you only like girls?"

She thought it over for a minute looking at the slight reflection of him in the window, where the darker shadow of the trees created a mirror effect. "I don't think that's any of your business."

"You could be right. But it's a terrible waste, with a body like you've got - also when we carry out the operation we are to be seen as a loving couple so that people do not try and get friendly with us and interrupt what we plan to do. Do you understand me?"

She spun round on the seat, her skirt riding up as she did so, looking straight into his eyes asking. "That does not mean we have to be lovers - why don't you tell me when we are going to start practising, or training, or whatever you want to call it?"

He was looking at her legs as she instinctively pulled the hem of her skirt down.

He looked up at her "We will go downstairs in a minute, in the cellar there is one of our factories. But you must be careful, otherwise you will blow the whole street. After the event we need to go through plans for your return to Belfast, and then the day before the operation we will go through that in detail, that's roughly the schedule."

"So, when is the operation going to take place, and where?"

"Like I said, you will be told the day before. What I can tell you is that it will take place over the Easter weekend, you don't have to know any more than that at this stage."

She got up from her seat and was making her way towards the door, "Shall we make a start then?"

He caught her wrist and spun her around "Couldn't we wait a little while we have got plenty of time?"

For some reason she was not certain why she felt fearful, despite that she spoke strongly "I suppose you would like to lay me down on the bed, nothing doing ... I came over here for one purpose, and when I've done that perhaps I'll sleep a little easier at night ... and it won't be with you ... knowing that my sister and father..." she stopped as he tightened his grip on her, pulling her gently towards him.

At first, she struggled, then letting herself go limp she allowed him to pull her to him". He started to smile, just a flicker as his lips puckered at the edges. She kept her face quite still allowing herself to be pulled nearer to him, then she said, "Please don't. I don't want to, and I'm not going to!" The last words she said very firmly.

She was quite close to him, he took a small step nearer to her, he felt her relax and pulled her closer, letting his eyes wander over her body taking in the soft lines which her skirt and jumper did little to hide, "You look marvellous." The only comment he could make as he felt his own anticipation rising inside him.

As he continued drawing her to him she turned to face him, "Please don't!" She was not pleading – she was ordering him to stop,

He wasn't listening, if he was, he did not show it. He lifted his free hand to her shoulder enticing her gently towards him. He watched her tongue slide across her lips leaving them shiny and moist he was not to know it was because she was nervous.

His heart started pounding at their softness, he glanced down at her body arching towards him. He leant forward to kiss her. Abruptly she leant backwards her right hand, which was by her side, came sweeping up in an arch and the flat of her hand slapped him hard across the face.

He let go of her stepping back holding one hand to his hurt cheek to ease the pain with a total look of shock on his face. Grousing as the sting from the palm of her hand swept through him in waves, creating a loud noise in is ear.

She moved out of his grasp saying . "I told you not to, but you wouldn't listen." Although she spoke clearly, she wasn't certain if he could hear her. As she looked at him, she was frightened at what he might do to her when he started to recover. She spun round and decided to go downstairs and wait for him, at least there would be company down there.

When he finally came down the stairs, he looked white and drawn, the finger marks of her hand still prominent on his cheek. "That bloody hurt, you bitch, if we didn't have a use for you or if there was time to change things, you'd be out, as it is - don't think I'll forget it in a hurry."

He took hold of her hand and pulled her towards the cellar, adding "You had better watch your step."

She dragged her arm away from him shouting, "I can walk without being pulled along."

As they reached the bottom of the steps, he stopped her, "Now listen, and listen carefully, whilst you are down here be bloody careful, otherwise one wrong move and the place could disappear. I'm going to show you the bombs we intend using, and then I'm going to explain what will set those bombs off, afterwards we will go back upstairs, and I'll tell you the rest of the planning. Now whatever you do, don't touch anything unless you are told to, is that clear?"

She nodded her head in agreement, she could see where the tears had been in his eyes and was regretting what she had done.

He led her over to a work bench where two metal beer kegs were lying on their side, wedges of wood on either side stopping them from rolling.

There was a naked bulb over the bench throwing a pool of light, leaving most of the corners in darkness. Next to the barrels were two timing devices, neatly laid out with the batteries standing to the back, a middle-aged man she had seen around the house was working with a soldering iron on one of the clocks.

"Now, I'm showing you this because I believe that if you know what happens when you do your part, you'll be just that bit better at it."

She nodded her head, but found it difficult to take her eyes off the two barrels, "Will they have the explosives put into them?"

"They are already loaded. The timing devices will be in your handbag and when you press the button, we will have two powerful bombs." He repeated himself. "Two very powerful bombs, enough to kill some of their bloody Army."

"Obviously, I cannot carry those two beer barrels...so how do I set them off?" She looked at him in surprise.

He couldn't help smiling, just being near the bombs made him happy, but to see them treated in awe was almost bliss.

"No, we will plant the bombs, but because of the location we need someone to plant the timing device, and that's where you come in."

"What do you mean, 'Because of the location?'"

"They will be planted in the cellar of a public house, for various reasons we cannot just put a normal timing device..."

"Why not?" She had a questioning look on her face.

"Because we are not certain what time the prey will be there." Her eyes were looking brightly into his, he waited for her to say something, when she didn't, he carried on. "Also, because they are below ground level, if we tried to operate them with a radio signal from outside the premises they may not work. That's where you come in."

"So, what am I supposed to do?" Because he was being so moderate and placid as he described what the operation was about, she could not help feeling a little guilty at the marks on his face and wanted to reach forward and stroke them. Then she added "I'm sorry for what I did earlier."

He turned, seeing her in a new light, somehow, she was different and affected him in different ways.

He pushed it to the back of his mind and continued with the project "As I said, the bombs will be in place the day before you and I visit the target in the evening. We will appear to be just a young couple enjoying a meal and holding hands – you get the picture."

Frances was nodding her head. "The restaurant is over the cellar, so we will have a meal and when the Army people arrive you will press a button on a small radio device which will in itself be timed, you will set it, and we will leave, very slowly arm in arm." he was pointing to the two items on the work bench

"And it will activate the bombs?" she was looking at them in awe.

"Of course they will." He sighed in exasperation and continued, wondering if they had the right person for the operation, he picked up one of the units and was pointing to the various control devices

"There are three controls. First a safety switch, the second is this triangular button, you do not need to touch that it regulates the time between pressing the button and when the bomb explodes, it is set for fifteen minutes." He looked at her to see if she was following "You do understand, because if you change it, it will activate the units in the cellar at a different time?"

She nodded her head and he continued. "The third item is this silver button. So, you operate the switch that will put the item in a ready state. Do not touch the timing regulator. After that when the time is right and the Army are in place you press the button, we will then have fifteen minutes to leave the place before the explosion."

She was staring at the two bombs smiling and nodding her head saying "I understand, the timing devices are to be in my hand bag and all I need to do is switch them on, and then wait until the Army are in place and when they are press the button and we both leave, that's right isn't it?"

She could feel her heart beating faster just being close to him wondering what it would have been like if she had not resisted him a little earlier.

"That's right, one will go off just a little time after the other, come we have some other things to talk about."

He had taken hold of her arm "Please don't keep pulling me about." She wriggled her arm free from him although she enjoyed him touching her.

After going into further details with her, an hour later he was about to leave, as he put on his coat he looked at her stopping what he was doing while he spoke, "I haven't forgotten what you did earlier, I'll put that matter right another time."

The look in his eyes frightened her, she was wishing she had found another way to resist him, she went to hold him but he dismissed her saying "Go over those instructions so that you know them and are word perfect, I'll see you in a couple of days and I'll be asking you to tell me what you have to do." He paused letting his eyes look her over before continuing. "The following Saturday we will be going to the project for the first time."

The door slammed behind him. As he left she felt very lonely as if part of her had gone with him. At first she was going to go to another room where the couple who lived there were, but the thought of company, who hardly said a word put her off - she turned and ran up the stairs, where she flung herself on the bed and started to sob. Suddenly she felt without a friend in the world and wished it had been different and she had laid with him."

The Chancer

In the early nineteen forties when the Second World War raged around Great Britain, with enemy bombers attacking in their swarms and causing disorder and chaos to each of the cities in the British Isles .

In a busy part of Guildford on the corner of a main road, stood a large furniture store, with a stunning eye-catching façade, called Donaldson's after the owner, who was a man in his sixties.

He was a person, although a regular visitor to the church, however, earlier in his youth he had shunned family life and set out to make money.

Richard, frequently shortened to Dick was an exceptional person in that he strived to keep his independence, and shunned company.

On the top floor of his store, which had been built in the Victorian period, around the eighteen thirties, was a large comfortably furnished flat. This is where he spent most of his time, when he was not attending to the needs of his business in the substantial show room on the ground floor, with its generous size of space.

It was Autumn and late evening, he was sitting at his desk, going through the figures in the accounts, when the first wailing of an air raid warning siren sounded. After months of the familiar noise warning of an attack which sometimes did not happen, he took little notice and continued what he was doing.

In the distance he could hear gun fire perpetrated by the ground forces trying to repel the attackers.

As time went past and the raid continued, he looked up as he had become aware the air intrusion was coming closer to where he was sitting.

There was the detonation of an exploding bomb close by, the flash from the discharge lighting up the window frame where the blackout curtain did not quite fit.

He quickly left the room and retired to the spot under the stairs, which he had previously made comfortable for such an event.

Although he had heard the initial whistle of the bomb which penetrated the centre of the furniture store, hurtling through it and finally exploding in the basement, Richard knew nothing of it as it had demolished the stairway.

The following blaze consumed the building and the fire officer, who was overwhelmed by the amount of destruction the bombers were creating that night, instructed his men to abandon Donaldson's to its fate and try to save other buildings which were not so badly damaged.

It was a few years after the war had come to an end, when the City Council took on the task of trying to link damaged properties, where the occupier was missing, to their rightful owner or relatives, however no matter how much they tried it was not possible to find a person who was related to Richard Donaldson.

What was left of the unsupported structure of windowless brickwork standing as a memorial to its past glory, was deemed to be unsafe and was pulled down at the Councils expense, and the site levelled and cleared.

Harry Cox's father had been a car trader before the hostilities. With the strict restrictions on the use of cars at the start of the war, brought his activities in his endeavours to earn a living by this means, to an end, especially more so when the Army required his services in a foreign land from which he did not return.

Now, the War was over and the horrors of it were becoming a distant memory, his son, Harry Cox was not one to miss an opportunity.

Over a period of time he watched the area being cleared, and now the last of the council's plant was leaving the site and the final lorry of rubble was being taken away. He lost no time in getting in touch with a friend and between them they moved two of the cars from his father's old stock, which had been residing in a barn, since before the war.

Cleaning them throughout so they sparkled and also trying to hide any rust, they moved them to the empty plot where they put a for sale sign on them. In the years after the war was a period when there was a heavy demand for cars, as there were very few new ones being produced for the home market, trade in the second hand market for used cars was brisk.

Time drifted past and to Harry's surprise no one questioned the use he had put the valuable location to, and as his confidence grew, he erected an office and finally a brick structure.

He had one problem and that was the lack of electric energy to work the lights, and as he was not too certain of the tenure he had on the property, he did not want to go to the heavy cost of putting power lines in.

One morning he arrived to find the Local Authority was installing new street lighting. To achieve this, they had dug deep trenches close to the boundary of the car plot to install the electric cables.

Harry looked at the work and had an idea. After talking to another one of his buddies, who was in the know about electricity, they came to a decision.

One Sunday afternoon when no Council work was being carried out on the lighting, a small gang of men made a connection to the new facility that was being installed, and ran a cable to the office of the car sales, disguising the work they had carried out so that it would not be seen.

With some trepidation, Harry waited for the new street lighting to be activated, and when it was, to his total surprise, he pressed a switch and he had electricity.

And now some time since selling his first car from the site, the place was a blaze of colour from its neon lighting declaring in giant red letters Harry's Car Lot and a row of shining cars, lined up on the front, with bright plastic stickers showing the price and other details.

It was the week before the Easter break, and Harry watched as two people entered the site and was looking at one of the American cars, which he specialised in.

He left them for a little while to see if they were really interested. Dressed in a smart grey tailored suit, he went out to speak to them.

The punter was opening the door of the Chevrolet Impala and peering inside the gleaming vehicle. Harry was walking slowly to them wondering if they had a car to part exchange, and what make and year it would be.

The clatter of the outside telephone bell shook him out of his thoughts. Returning to the office he picked up the instrument, and immediately recognised who the caller was.

"Hello Harry, we missed you at the game last weekend, and what do you know that bloody Calvin, whatever his other name is, kept winning the pot – would you believe it?"

"The trouble is Charlie, I do believe it, I've can't help feeling, and I am sure others feel the same, he is cheating somehow."

"Well some of us want to take him to the cleaners and we are hoping you will be there to help – what do you say?"

"Look Charlie, I have a punter on that piece of junk of a Yank, which I have regretted ever having bought it as I paid too much money for it, so I must go ... is the game going to be at the usual place and time?"

"Yeah, seven thirty in the Casino at The Black Rose, I have been ringing round and I think we will have a full house, as all the team will be there, see you Saturday." Harry was putting the phone down when he heard the other speaking "We thought we would meet in the bar for a livener first"

"That is fine with me, now I must go as they are crawling over the car, I've got a feeling they are going to buy it."

"In that case the first round will be on you. See you Saturday."

Harry went back out to hopefully sell the vehicle. After taking the couple who were excited about the car, for a demonstration ride, they returned to the office where they parted with their money, and as the new owners drove away in their purchase, harry Cox clapped his hands.

~~~

At the Black Rose they were preparing the function room for the Mayors and his Party for the Saturday evening Party.

In South East London a bomb was being prepared.

~~~

Liz & Christopher

The alarm in the small bedsit shrilled as the mechanism clicked over on the hour of seven, allowing the tightly coiled spring to unwind, setting the bell off in a jangle demanding that the sole occupant of the room awaken.

Elisabeth, who much preferred to be called the shortened name of Liz, stretched herself under the covers and extended a slim arm out in the search of the offending noise.

Her finger pressed a button restoring silence to the room. For a moment she lay there tempted to go back to her dream world, but like every other morning she threw the covers back and raised her slim form to sit on the edge of the bed, wiping the sleep from her eyes.

As she looked around the room, its neatness marred by the cheap old furniture supplied by the

Landlord, whose one aim was to keep the cost down of renting out the property.

A small shudder ran down her back as she compared it to her parents' home above the Public House they owned.

However, three years previously, at the age of eighteen, she had decided to move away and live her own life, and make her home nearer to her place of work.

The drab grey mottled curtains hung depressingly at the window, which showed an even more depressing day outside with a fine misty rain creating small rivulets running down the window pane.

Liz shivered slightly and reached for her dressing gown, which once adorned, effectively hid her figure in its quilted folds.

As she prepared her breakfast she thought of the day ahead at the bank in the centre of Guildford.

For four years she had been one of twelve cashiers. In the previous twelve months she had been promoted, and now worked, along with the head of staff, to assure the branches cash levels were adequate, and there were sufficient staff to guarantee a swift and outstanding service to the clients.

She started out to her place of work in the usual bus, seeing the same familiar faces – none of whom she knew as they were complete strangers to her.

Every morning was the same, as all of them seemed to spend the journey swapping stares at each other, and no doubt each wondering what their day would bring.

The scruffy looking red double decked means of transport ground to a halt, it's growling engine throbbed throughout the vehicle.

It was the normal struggle to board the vehicle amongst the others trying to find a seat before the bell indicated the bus was starting to move.

The usual passengers who got off at the same stop as Liz, stood up from their seats forming a ragged queue and tightly packed together struggled to the exit.

Once inside the large Georgian structure, standing in a row of similar buildings, which had been supplying banking facilities to the local community for a very long time.

Liz made her way to the staff room greeting her colleagues and catching up with the current gossip and the previous evenings television.

Then the familiar duties of the day began, preparing the bureau for nine thirty when the first customers would be allowed access to the tills.

The door behind the cashiers run opened; Liz glanced over her shoulder to see the assistant manager, Christopher Perkins coming up to her. "Good morning Miss Hallard, are we ready for the day's onslaught?"

Her heart gave a little leap as he came up to her "Good morning, Sir. Yes, I think so."

She looked at him her mind flashing back to the time when he had called her into his office. She had wondered what it was for and was surprised when he asked if she would go out to dinner one evening, which she had accepted.

It was only over the meal on that initial meeting did she start to wonder why she had accepted the invitation, as she knew he was married also knowing that the association could not possibly lead anywhere.

They had become lovers a few evenings later, a relationship which she found pleasing and not easy to hide during the day. It was something exceedingly difficult to conceal from the remainder of the staff, who would nod at each other in a knowing way whenever he went near to speak to her.

Liz, who was thinking it did not seem that long ago he had slipped out of her bed kissing her on the nose, as was his habit before disappearing home to his wife.

Having completed his morning rounds, Chris returned to his office to deal with matters of the day.

During his career in the bank, he had had numerous affairs with different girls in the various branches where he had worked. They all had followed the same pattern, and if his wife knew, then she was not prepared to refer to them or do anything about it.

This time it was different, he was more involved, and he had started to take risks He suspected rather than knew, that their closeness was common knowledge by the staff, who all were guessing at a deeper relationship.

His excesses in his lifestyle had led to financial difficulties. The year previously, with his position of authority, he had transferred funds for his own use.

It was a move he constantly regretted because he could not replace them without being found out – if he didn't return them he would still be discovered when the branch audit took place, which could be at any time in a five year frame work.

He was between the devil and the deep blue sea and could only let events take their course.

He often thought of perpetrating a large fraud on one of the large accounts knowing that once his misdeed had been discovered, his career would be at an end. He was vastly aware he would be discovered at some time. He was now looking for an alternative so when the day of reckoning came, he would not be without funds and some form of future.

In many ways he regretted the moment of madness, as he knew he would be sorry to lose the respect and the authority which he held.

However, being a practical man, he realised there was no going back when he had undertaken the deception. Although he was unhappy about what would happen to his wife, the thought of a new and different life with Liz, paled everything else and made it nonexistent.

He would go tomorrow if everything was in place and although he had never discussed it with her, he knew she would come … his one problem was money, somehow he would find a way so that the bank would supply him with enough cash to make life with the girl he loved, comfortable.

To this end he spent most of his days concentrating on ways to achieve this without raising suspicion. Although during the day he had found the time to talk to his new love, he had also arranged to meet her later.

Removing the security chain from the front door of the bank signified the end of the day for Elisabeth. Saying "Goodnight" to the remainder of the staff she ventured out into the wet early evening weather, struggling with her umbrella trying to hold it against the wind gusting around the corner of the tall building.

The pitter patter of the rain finding the roof of her brolly, before they ran down the sides falling from the edge to the ground in large drops. If Liz was unlucky, they fell onto the back of her nylon covered legs, sending a small shiver up her back, as she made her way to the bus stop.

As was her habit in the cold inclement weather, she would promise herself to take driving lessons. She was thinking it would not be too long before she could settle down with Chris as he had promised many times. Perhaps he would teach her to drive – she would like that. She had a vision of an open top car, the sun beating down and the man she loved coaching her into being an expert driver.

Tonight, she had agreed to play badminton with him at the leisure centre on the outskirts of town. Liz was very fond of Chris, she would almost say she was in love with him.

However, she could not see much future in the relationship unless he got the divorce he frequently promised would happen. She liked the idea of being the wife of a bank manager. Tonight, she would bring the subject up to see how he reacted.

The soft throbbing of the big diesel engine could be heard from the big red double decke bus as it splashed along the gutter to pull up at the stop, which made Liz and the rest of the queue step back as the water washed over the pavement, forced there from the big road wheels of the vehicle.

Shuffling along she boarded the means of transport automatically paying her fare before finding a seat. Tired but excited, in half an hour she would be at the place she called home, and an hour later she would be with Chris.

She finally got to the venue for their game and saw him standing beside the courts dressed in whites – she waved and ran to the ladies rooms to change, emerging a few minutes later adorned in her sports attire, fitting snugly to her trim figure. They hugged briefly and made their way to the courts swinging their rackets as they did so.

"You are late." He chided.

"The rotten taxi which I ordered, was very late, in fact at one time I didn't think it was ever going to turn up – and when it did I think the driver fancied me, he drove very slowly and tried to chat me up."

"I admire his taste ... I'll let you go first." Using his racquet, he flipped the shuttlecock to her as he said it.

"You are asking to be thrashed tonight!" as she caught the item and made her way to her end of the court.

"Well, I can't keep winning, you may not want to play with me anymore." He was grinning and preparing for her to serve to him.

"I shouldn't worry too much about that as I can't wait for this game to finish." Smiling at him and seeing his sharp reaction as she flipped the feathered orb into the air.

An hour later both pleasantly tired and relaxed they walked hand in hand from the court, letting a foursome, who had booked the facility after them, play. Going up a short set of stairs they made their way towards the bar. "Do you fancy a drink?" He asked her.

"Pleeease ... I'm so thirsty. Anyway, it is the first time I have beaten you at badminton ... so a little one to celebrate ... second thoughts make it half a lager, I am too thirsty for anything smaller."

She smiled up at him admiring the rugged face with the sparkling blue eyes. "I'll go and sit over there in the corner." As Liz was saying it she was nodding her head in the direction of an empty table.

Returning from the bar he placed the drink in front of her, the froth from the top spilling down the side of the glass on to the tabletop.

He sat down pulling his chair close to her and taking hold of her hand. "Chris...can I ask you something?" quickly he knew this was going to be a question he did not like.

"Of course, you can, but don't sound so serious...now what is the problem?"

"Well, it is serious...very serious." She paused looking at him with an unsmiling look on her face. "What is going to happen to us?"

He smiled at her squeezing her hand before replying. "What would you like to happen?"

"More than we have got now. I want to wake up in the morning to find you there. I want you to confirm what you have told me so many times, that you are leaving your wife and getting divorced ... I want to start making plans."

She stopped getting her breath and looking at him in the face.

He looked at her seriously not knowing what to say before she continued.

"I want to know that when my holiday comes around, I am going to be with you instead of sitting around all day waiting for you to finish at the office before I can see you. I do not want to suffer the pangs of jealousy when you go away taking your wife with you, leaving me to wonder and wait..." a tear had formed in the corner of her eyes.

He was nodding his head and squeezed her hand a little tighter. Her eyes flared in a frustrated anger as she looked straight into his eyes.

"You do understand, don't you Chris?"...she waited for a response, but none came.

"I want more ... not now, but a firm date when this half existence will be over. I want you to verify what you have said too many times for it to be believable ... about the divorce you were going to start, so that we can be together."

Declan O'Donnell

The two men had arranged to meet so as to discuss the details of the proposed operation. They arrived outside The Black Rose just after noon and dressed smartly as two businessmen they went into the Saloon Bar where they sat at a table in an almost empty room.

They spoke quietly so as not to be overheard. "So Lewis, what do you think of Frances?"

"She'll do, a little bit old fashioned, but with the new clothes she will be alright, I've been bringing her here as agreed."

"Have you got any problems with her – now remember what I told you, none of your sadistic ways, we don't want her looking worse for wear."

Lewis shrugged his shoulders and looked around the bar as if the other was being a bore. "Okay, I hear what you say, but she is a bit fanciful."

"Let's move on ... have the kegs been organised?"

"Yes, that is done and finished and waiting to be moved" He paused, the other looked at him expectantly. "There is a little problem with designing the mechanism to activate them, but I'm told that will be solved very shortly."

"What's the problem, there is not a lot of time before the operation?" he looked at his companion with a serious look.

"As I understand it there are two. The first is the need for two bombs, which means carrying two sets of firing buttons, and they are a bit unwieldy."

"There has to be two, in case one does not go off and the other reason it is a big building we want it raised to the ground – what's the other problem?"

"Just the size of them as they both must have a switch, because if there was just a button on its own there is the risk it could be activated by mistake. If there was just one then it would be a lot easier, because two are a bit bulky to carry into a restaurant."

"That is why we are using a woman nobody questions what they have in their handbag. Anyway, as I just said we need two just in case one does not fire, also as I said, it is a large place one may not be enough." He paused and looked around him before adding. "The only other thing is how do you plan to deliver them?"

"Shaun with the help of Eddie has that organised, he understands the delivery schedule of beer and other supplies, and I am told he has worked out a method of getting them into the cellars."

Declan was nodding his head, "That's good they are capable people and I am sure they know what they are doing. The issues you have raised I do not see them as a reason for delaying the operation and I do not see why it should not go ahead." Shortly after the pair parted company and went their individual ways.

~~~

At the Black Rose they continued to prepare the function room for the Mayors Party.

In South East London a bomb was nearing completion.

~~~

Liz & Christopher

Christopher was shocked; they were still seated in the bar near to the badminton courts. He had always known that sooner or later he would have to make a decision, and for some reason he could not understand why the problem had come to a head at this time. He sat looking at her not knowing what to say, "Don't worry, everything will work out fine."

"Nothing will work out unless you do what you have said you are going to ... and you have said it on many occasions, especially when you are feeling randy and want to get me into bed."

He could see the anger in her eyes and realised that he should have seen the situation developing but he had been so intent on her company and his other problems, that he had not realised how she considered their relationship,

"Darling" he felt her pull her hand away, he faltered before continuing "It's just that we have never discussed it before, and you have always seemed content with our arrangement that...." he had run out of words, and tried to break the spell by leaning over to kiss her.

She moved back, "No! Please finish."

"No, not here – look, let's go and get changed and discuss it over dinner." He had started to stand up.

"You are trying to avoid the issue." Liz knew that if she didn't keep the momentum up, she would not be as positive if she allowed him to talk her into a cooling off period.

"I'm not, I promise you, we will discuss our future over dinner tonight, not here where..."

"Where what...oh never mind, I'll see you downstairs." With that she stood up and flounced towards the changing rooms.

Chris tried to break the mood that had come between them as they drove towards the restaurant. He had known that sooner or later he would have to face reality, he had put the moment off time and time again, and now Liz was demanding an answer.

In his heart he wanted to live with his new love and leave his wife and three children. However, it was a big step to take. It was obvious that Elisabeth wanted to live with him, but how would she react when she discovered the fraud he had perpetrated on the bank.

A silence had come between them, and yet somehow it was creating a bond that was demanding communication, both wanting to tell the other how they felt, and yet neither wanting to be the first to speak

Elisabeth was in a sombre mood and was looking out of the car window watching the lights outside reflecting from the various shop front windows, she could feel the heater blowing warm air around her feet.

Yet her mind was trying to sort out her life, she wanted to be able to say to Chris that she loved him and wanted to hold him, but she did not want to continue living in this hell. Now that she had brought the subject up, she was strong minded to see it through until she had an answer.

She was also just as determined that she was not going to open the conversation, she wanted to see if he was serious about discussing the future.

They had stopped at a set of lights when Chris spoke, "I thought we would go to that little Italian Restaurant."

She smiled to herself as she answered, "If you wish." Feeling she had won the first round.

He was trying to break the atmosphere that had developed between them and continued speaking "There is so much I want to tell you...I'm not certain where to begin," The car started to move forward as the traffic lights turned to green.   There followed another deep embarrassing silence between them as Chris struggled with his conscience.

"Chris, why don't you just come out with what you are going to say?" She flung the question at him.

He spoke softly "What you are saying, is that the moment of truth has come, and you want me to make a decision, either you or my wife and family."

"Put like that, the answer is yes." Her voice was hard, she could feel her temper getting short.

There was no immediate reply, she let out a long sigh and resumed looking at the shop fronts with their reflected glass, the water on the car window creating patterns of lights, as the rain, caught in the slip stream, flowed past them.

He knew he had to say something to try and break the tension. "I've often thought about it, but...." he shrugged his shoulders.

Liz glared at him "But what? Shrugging your shoulders will not help."

He glanced at her "But...well that's just about as far as I've got."

"What thinking about it ... have you considered how I feel?" she had raised her voice and was regretting ever agreeing to go out with him.

"Of course, I have, but you have not mentioned it before." He was stuttering over his words.

"Oh Chris!" She sighed and looked at him sharply "What do you mean I haven't mentioned it before. What do you think I do every time we meet? Or do you think the nights you don't see me I've got somebody else as a sort of standby, what do you think I am Chris?"

Liz was getting exasperated, she felt like going home, as the feeling of depression was sweeping over her. She glanced across at him, at the same time he tried to hold her hand as was his habit when they were in the car, she pulled her hand away, determined to get some form of commitment from him.

"If it wasn't for the children, it would be so much easier."

"Well, it's certain you can't have both, so one way or another you are going to have to make up your mind and make a choice, me or them."

"What do you want me to do?" He had looked at her feeling helpless and wondering how he was going to calm her down.

"I think you had better let me out of the car, because I'm not getting through to you."

"Why would you want to do that....." Nevertheless, he decided to stop.

She had started to laugh, for suddenly the whole situation was too stupid, and as quickly as she had started to laugh, she found herself wanting to cry. She took a long look at him, fighting back the tears, barely noticing the car stopping as he pulled into the kerb.

As he was putting the hand brake on he turned and smiled at her, "You are very pretty."

The whole scene was too much for Liz, she burst into tears, scrabbling through her bag trying to find a tissue.

He took a folded white handkerchief from his top pocket and offered it to her, she at first pushed it away, but then relented when she was unable to find what she wanted.

She looked up at him, he was still smiling, she didn't want him to smile she wanted him to be meaningful. Why couldn't he be serious? Why wouldn't he tell her what she wanted to hear? She waited, waiting for him to say something.

Abruptly it was all too much, she opened the car door as the tears started to pour down her face.

The rain lashed at her, but she was not aware of it, she wanted to be as far away as possible from him and that car.

He had to wait for the traffic before he could open the door, then he was out of the car.

He was not certain where she had gone and looked around him and saw her chasing along the road in the direction they had come from.

Ignoring getting very wet he called her name, running hard trying to catch up with her.

Her feet were soaking and soggy where she had run through and ignored the puddles. The rainwater was running down her neck, but she did not care, she wanted to get away from him.

She could hear him chasing, she tried that much harder she did not want him near her.

Suddenly he caught her by the arm and turned her round in the same movement, she half fell as her feet slipped, he held on stopping her from falling to the ground.

They looked at each other briefly, water running down their faces, the rain mixing with her tears.

It seemed like an age while they stood there, they began to smile at each other. His lips were searching for hers.

She started to laugh, and then they both had the giggles with the rain falling harder than before.

The following days were bliss for Liz, at long last Chris, had made a commitment to her, he had promised to discuss the whole thing with his wife, and tell her he was leaving, in the mean time Liz was to find somewhere where they could both live and be together.

She had started studying the local paper looking for a flat, somewhere that would be the start of their new life, until they could look for something more permanent.

It was good to get up in the morning, and although she had always taken care of the way she looked, she now took that additional care. Her voice was more lighthearted which reflected laughter, and she burst into a big smile at the simplest thing.

It was a few evenings later, they had been playing badminton again, and had managed the corner seat in the bar, "Chris, I'm so happy, I feel excited about the place I'm going to look at tomorrow."

She had described it to him before the game, so he was able to answer. "It does sound just right."

He took her hand, almost out of habit, "The owners bank with us, I'll give them a ring in the morning and put in a good word for you."

Her face for a moment went sad, "Don't you mean for us." She looked at him sharply.

"Of course, I do, but you know what I mean?" he was feeling embarrassed in some way he could not get used to the thought of living with her.

Liz was nodding her head "I think so, when are you going to tell her.?"

"When y...we have got a place to live in, which now seems it could be soon."

She threw her arms around him, "Darling, I'm so happy, I want to tell Mum and Dad, let's go over there one night."

Chris was not too happy at that suggestion, he still did not know how he was going to break the news to his wife, and yet somehow, he knew he was going to have to.

Perhaps it would be easier if he had somewhere to go with this beautiful girl, and for certain if he was going to carry on seeing her, he was going to have to make the break.

"Darling, what are you thinking of...?" She was sipping her drink and smiling at him.

"Nothing really...I was looking forward to our own place." Somehow the words did not seem real or honest. She didn't seem to notice for she squeezed him some more. '

"Next week it's a good night down at the pub."

"What do you mean, why would next week be a better night then any others?"

"Well, what I mean" she replied laughing, "Next Saturday is a good night down the pub, they have a party, there will be a professional act and after people get on the stage singing and telling jokes and things..." He had started to laugh at her, "Don't laugh..."

"It's just that you look so happy." His heart welled up and he knew she was the person he wanted to live with. "Well, you said it and I am! Next week, I will have my new flat, you will come and live with me, and I'm going to one of Mum's parties."

When he left her that night, he knew that somehow he was going to have to pluck up the courage to tell his wife of his intentions, as events were starting to move extremely fast.

~~~

The finishing touches were being added to the Black Rose function room which was nearing completion for the Party Night.

In a cellar in South London there was agreement that the priming devise for the two beer keg bombs worked.

~~~

Bar Games Ltd

Brian Arthur Roberts, the Managing Director of BAR GAMES LTD, the name being derived from his own initials, was seated at his desk which was strewn with paper. He was doodling with a fibre tip pen, while he thought out the next move in his bid to obtain the manufacturing rights which had been offered in that month's trade press. As he pondered, he knew he had done all he could and now it was a matter of waiting.

He desperately needed a new facility to boost lagging production, to give the factory a better chance to grow. Of late, he had wondered many times how and why he had gone in for manufacturing games. Not being able to remember what influenced him so many years before.

The industry by the very nature of it was so volatile, because of the design stage and production times with tooling problems, before the finished items could be transported from the factory to their retail outlets. As a result, he and his management team were constantly trying to judge what the market would require in eighteen months time.

As a going concern which had all its capital tied up, plus a loan from the bank, they badly needed an item that could be manufactured on a continuing basis, to level the troughs in their working cycle so as to gives the Company stability.

It was such an opportunity that was now being offered, but he knew a few other manufacturers, in the same position as himself, would be bidding for the prospect.

His wife Sarah, who doubled as his secretary during the day, opened his office door, slightly startled he looked up.

For a moment she was framed in the doorway her once slim figure now spreading, the young, youthful look on her face being replaced by tired worry lines.

He abruptly realised what the years had done to them. The dreams were turning into a treadmill of worry; the only glimmer of hope was to constantly look for a door to open that would lead to riches.

"Yes love?" his customary answer when she came into his office.

"We have a mysterious visitor outside. He says his name is Ken Williams."

Looking slightly puzzled he asked, "What does he want?"

"He says he wants to see you, and to quote him, 'To your fiscal advantage'"

"What's he selling, life insurance?" it was the first thought that came into his head.

"No, I've been through that hoop, he says he can help in 'landing a new facility', as he puts it."

Brian was puzzled and looked it. He smiled up at his wife "Did he say what sort of new facility?"

She shook her head, by way of an answer. He sat there for a few minutes thinking.

All of a sudden, the office, despite its modern appearance and furnishing appeared to him in its true state, untidy even dirty, the dust laying on the venetian blinds a monument to how he had allowed the deterioration to take place.

His hesitation confirmed in his own mind the depth he had reached.

A few years before he would have made an instant decision whether to see the man: or not. Now he could not recognise the difference between an opportunity and grasping at straws.

What did he have to lose? If he didn't take some form of action, the Banks confidence in him would decline and then all their efforts to make the business viable would come to nothing.

At thirty six he was too tired to start again, to go through all the inconvenience of setting up a new business and making it work? He had to see this man, whatever he had to offer was better than sitting doing nothing and hoping that tomorrow would take care of itself.

As he looked up at her she saw the indecision in his face, wishing she could help but not knowing how.

Taking one quick look round the untidiness, he said, "You had better wheel him in and see what he has to offer,"

Williams practically bounced into the office, his immaculate dark blue suit and impeccable clothing, making Brian feel even more dowdy as he stood up to shake his hand. He made a mental promise to himself that he would have to change his ways and project a better image.

"Mr Roberts, I'll come straight to the point, as I understand it you are in a position where you have capacity for extra manufacturing facilities. Is that correct?"

Brian reached across the desk to retrieve his pipe, seeking its comfort in front of this youngster; silence hung in the room, while he considered how to answer the questioner, lighting the pipe while he did so.

"Every manufacturer would like to increase their capacity." He was staring at his visitor with a grin hovering around his mouth.

The visitor was also grinning as he made himself comfortable in a chair "But with respect, yourself more than most."

Brian, a proud man who was not liking this interview, which was rapidly being controlled by this smooth almost brash young man who had to be at least ten years his junior.

Trying to keep the conversation low key, he replied quietly, "I'm not certain what you are driving at, but what the position of the company is at the present time is not your concern, but the concern of the Directors."

"Mr Roberts, I did not mean to sound offensive. I was merely stating facts. As I understand the position, you and your wife, the only Directors of the Company, have a factory only producing half of its capacity, is that true?"

Brian recognised the reference to Directors for what it was, to show he had done his homework on their situation.

"It would be foolish of me to admit that by increasing production it would not be of help." As he said it, he knew he was getting the worst of the conversation, and he must try and find a way to turn the situation to his advantage.

"I'm pleased you said that because at least we can come to an understanding, and therefore not waste each other's time. With that in mind I'm sure I can be of assistance to you."

"How?" As he spat out the one syllable word, he could feel the excitement running through him. He tried to show that he was not really concerned and deliberately took time to light his pipe again.

"Mr Roberts, you are aware that there is a manufacturer with an excess capacity problem who is looking for a reliable company to take this excess off his hands so as to satisfy the market requirements. You yourself have tendered for that business, is that not true?"

Brian puffed at his pipe, nodding his head in agreement but not wishing to interrupt.

"If I was to tell you that I was in a position to help you land that contract, on perhaps more favourable terms than you have already intimated that you are prepared to undertake the work for, I guess you would be interested to listen."

"I'd be a fool not to." Brian was looking at his visitor and showing interest although still supporting his pipe clamped between his teeth.

"Then that would only leave one problem, what would be my reward for creating such a facility for you?"

Very quickly he became annoyed and spoke sharply "Young man, you breeze into my office with some wild offer, and start asking for rewards on the assumption that you can create additional work for my factory. Now that's all fine in theory, but where are the facts to back it up. Who are you? How did you know that we had tendered for certain work? Furthermore, why approach this Company or are you doing the rounds to see what is the best deal you can get for yourself, assuming of course you can do what you say you can?"

The other was taken aback by the others strong words, "Mr Roberts, let me be frank with you. I hope I can speak in confidence because what I'm going to say, and providing you act on it, will be of benefit to you."

Brian, still puffing on his pipe was creating a layer of smoke, he was trying to unsettle the other party with this action.

Nodding his head he said "I'm listening," and for the first time he realised that Mr Williams was nervous, as he had started to fiddle with a ring and was showing signs of stress.

"Quite honestly, you say you want to be frank – but frank about what – you must realise your very action is causing suspicion?"

"Yes, I am sorry, I have not handled things very well but let me come straight to the point – you are right, - there are other firms which have applied and I, as an outside consultant - have been asked to evaluate each one."

He paused before continuing. "Quite frankly your organisation is the only one in which - in my opinion - could cope with the work that is being offered." He was talking in small blocks and he knew he was not putting his case very well.

Brian looked at his watch, "So you could be the cavalry coming to my rescue." Smiling he said. "You don't happen to have a white horse outside? Look it is nearly lunch time, why don't we go across to The Black Rose and continue our conversation there."

It was almost two hours later, and despite Brian Roberts protest, Ken was ordering a further round of brandies.

By now the pair had become very friendly and the owner of Bar Games Ltd was looking forward to the future with new confidence.

They were getting up to leave when Brian spoke.

"So, Ken, you will now go back to your people on the basis that you have looked into all the companies that have tendered, and that the contract should go to Bar Games Ltd." He paused for a short while mulling over the proposition in his mind.

"All you have got to do Brian, is open a banking account in our joint names; when I deliver the goods then my signature can be added to the account."

"I'm not certain why you want to become a Director of my company?"

"Brian, it's the only security that I have got, with a directorship you have to inform me what is going on, and it will give me recognition that a deal exists between us."

"But won't your people become suspicious?"

"Not really, they will see it as a protection of their interest, and I will explain that I took the step to the benefit of everyone. There is no argument about that. They will have the facility they want, you will have what you want, and I will have a brighter future."

"Okay! Where and when do we start?"

"I think Brian, without meaning to be offensive, you make a start by clearing the rubbish from the premises, and making the office look like the place of a successful business. That way when the big bosses pay a visit it will make them far happier.

Brian was trying to hide his embarrassment and nodding his head murmuring that he would make a start that afternoon.

Leaving Williams at the car park, allowing him to drive directly back to London, Brian walked to the factory.

He wanted to clear his head after the unusual heavy lunch. By the time he arrived he had made up his mind that it was time for a spring clean, and that the following day, instead of production, he would have the work force making the place sparkle. He would sort out the details of the proposal with Sarah, to take advantage of what was left of the afternoon.

Bouncing into the office, Sarah looked up and could hardly believe the transformation that had come over him, the old sparkle was in his eyes, and suddenly she knew that there was going to be a change from the slippery path they had been on.

Frances & Lewis

The days had passed slowly, and she knew exactly what she had to do. In reality there were not many things to remember, and in any case if anything did go wrong, or if she forgot something, there would be Lewis there to help.

Having read every book she could get her hands on, that were in the house, she watched the television, or most of the time looked out of the rear window, and watched the squirrels playing in the trees.

She had been told that he was expected that day. She was looking forward to seeing him with a thrill of expectation.

Frances had taken special care with her makeup, and had selected one of her new garments, a simple black cocktail dress the skirt of which barely touched her knees.

He finally returned, she heard him enter the house and talk to someone on the lower floor.

She wondered how important he might be inside the organisation; he was treated with respect and whatever he said no one argued with him. She heard him enter the room. Frances turned away from the window smiling.

"Hello Frances" He was also smiling "Do you know what you have got to do.?" His voice was soft and inquisitive.

She shrugged her shoulders, still smiling "There not much to it, is there?"

"You are right, be certain what there is, you get right." He sat on the other chair in the room, admiring her back as she turned to look out of the window.

He let his eyes meander over the shapely figure, the slim waist, the trim ankles, and then got annoyed with himself for wanting her.

When she had turned her back to him, he felt that she had insulted him, he wanted her to be friendly and pleasant.

"You still look at those bloody squirrels." He said sharply. She turned her face over her shoulder allowing a small smile to creep over her face "I think they are fascinating the way they jump from tree to tree, without a care in the world." "Why don't you come over here and I'll show you something really fascinating." He could feel the stirring of need in him.

She turned around to look at him "Are we at that again, you'll remember what happened last time."

She was smiling her eyes sparkling. "I am truly sorry for what I did, but I felt threatened." Her skirt had risen up and she pulled it down gently.

The urge to get up from where he was seated and take the few short steps to her, was strong, but the feeling of being made a fool of was even stronger. He was not going to let that happen again.

A silence had settled on the room, a stillness which they both found embarrassing. He watched with the feeling of the strong desires mounting in him.

She waited, not sure what to do. What he wasn't to know was that she had decided that whatever he wanted he could have.

If he was as important as she thought he was, it was not a good idea to make an enemy of him. Not only that, although it was a good enough reason, but for the first time in her life she wanted to lay with a man and this one in particular.

As the silence between them grew, she tried to change the mood, she fiddled with the hem of her skirt, his eyes followed what she was doing.

"You bitch, you are teasing me. I don't know whether to hurt you or to feed you to the English pigs."

Very quickly she felt very nervous and almost stuttered "Why would you want to do that?"

"Because you hurt me, nobody- but nobody does that and gets away with it."

She could feel herself starting to tremble, she had heard what had been done to people that had fallen out of favour.

She watched his eyes looking over her, the stare in them made her shudder, she wanted to go to him but did not know how.

"I have said I am sorry, and I do really mean it, in fact afterwards I wanted to stroke the hurt on your face to try and make it better."

"We could have done this the nice way the other day, but now I think you need a lesson taught to you. And it is going to be right now."

The fear continued spreading through her but the need for him was greater and she knew she was going to lay with a man for the first time and it was going to be very shortly.

Her hands had started to shake as she looked into his eyes, "You have no need to hurt me." She was shaking her head slowly.

He gulped, he had never had any respect for women, they were there, as far as he was concerned for his sexual pleasure.

But Frances was so different; she had a strong personality, an inner strength which he was finding difficult to define.

She was running her tongue over her lips although she was not aware of doing it as she had always done it when excited or nervous. He was not to know that and felt the blood rushing through him into his lower body.

She was leaning forward, her hands going up her back whilst smiling at him saying,

"Earlier on you said you were going to show me something fascinating..." Frances had located the long zip at the back of her dress and started to pull it downwards.

Lewis watched as the excitement swept through him as she slowly stood up sliding her arms out of the garment and lowering it down, displaying her breasts covered with a small white bra, before stepping out of the item of clothing.

His eyes swept over her now almost naked body. He released the braces from his shoulders and removed his trousers and then quickly his under garment.

Frances was stunned as she had never seen a man's strong and hard penis before. She watched in enthralment as he held it at its base.

She was trembling with anticipation. They both stood there admiring each other. The need for him was pulsing through her, her head in a spin as she watched him remove the remainder of his clothes.

A feeling of guilt was troubling her, because of the church's teaching about sex and marriage.

Nevertheless, she pushed it away, she was enjoying the excitement of this new world, standing nearly naked in front of a man and admiring his form and the lust radiating out of him knowing it was for her.

She quivered with excitement.

The normal action of lowering her skimpy knickers, took on a new meaning as he watched with a strange grin as she let them drop down to the floor.

As if by some signal Frances lay down on the bed still looking at his strong body in awe. She felt important a feeling she did not expect and watched as he knelt on the bed. A quivering swept through her.

With no more thought she waited in anticipation for what was to happen next.

~~~

In South London there were arrangements being made for the delivery of the bombs to their target

~~~

Bar Games

A few evenings later Sarah sat watching a soap opera, on the television. Since the advent of Ken Williams into their lives, she had hardly seen anything of Brian outside their place of work.

She normally left the office early to meet her three teenage boys from school, and to cook the evening meal. Over the past few weeks Brian had not arrived home until quite late, having grabbed a bite to eat on the way.

As the programme dragged on she knew that it was going to be another late evening, and with a shrug of her shoulders she rose from her chair and walked to the kitchen to turn the heat out under the saucepan that was keeping his meal hot.

In the lounge of the large detached house the usual noise was coming from the boy's recreation room, which was opposite the T.V room.

It was a house which Sarah loved. When they had first seen it, ten years previously, she had known that was where she had wanted to live.

It was off a country lane at the end of a long drive and not too far from the factory.

At the time it seemed large and the price much more than they wanted to pay, but she had wanted it so very much. At the time it had been touch and go whether they would buy it, but somehow they had managed it.

And now so many years later the property was worth far more than what they had paid for it, and they had turned down many offers for it.

With some they had been on the verge of accepting as the business worries had built up.

But they had never made a final decision to sell despite the enormous upkeep of the property. And now thanks to the contract that was about to be signed, it looked as if their financial worry would be removed and they would be able to carry out some much needed repair work, to their home.

Having given her customary shout to the boys to keep the noise down, she returned to the television to see the titles sliding across the screen as another episode finished.

It was then she heard the car in the drive, looking through the window she saw Brian's car pulling up outside the front door.

To her surprise he had brought company with him, which was exceptionally unusual.

She rushed out into the hall to tidy herself, taking her apron off as she ran up the stairs. On reaching the bedroom, she heard the front door open and the two men talking as they made their way to the lounge.

"This is some property you have here, Brian, it must be worth a small fortune."

"It's costly to keep up with though, it needs a lot doing to it now."

"Well you should be able to afford that soon, we will have that contract signed within the next few weeks, and then the money should start to flow."

Brian could not get used to somebody else using 'we' when talking about his business and was not certain if he would ever get used to it.

Mentally shrugging his shoulders he thought, what the hell, he was going to make more money out of this one deal than he had ever made, so if he had to give away twenty-five percent of the company to do so, it was still good business.

"Hello darling. Oh Ken, it is pleasant of you to come round and see us."

"Mrs Roberts, it is nice to see you again." Despite Sarah's pleading Ken still insisted on calling her by her surname, "I was just saying to your husband what a lovely home you have."

"Thank you. Would you like a cup of tea or something stronger?"

"If you have one - a scotch please, tea is really a morning drink."

"What about you Brian?" He was looking at her smiling "Thank you love, I'll have a scotch as well please." She went off to do their bidding.

"Right, let's get down to business, first Brian, have you ordered the new machinery?"

"Well, I have been wondering about that, they will require twenty five percent deposit and that is a lot of money, especially if this contract falls through."

"What do I need to do to convince you that it is not going to fall through...pass the ashtray please... it's as good as in your desk drawer now, or in the bank, or where ever you keep these things." .

"Perhaps I'm being over cautious but if it is only a matter of weeks before the contract is finalised I don't see why we shouldn't wait until then, at least we will be certain and we will not have committed ourselves to spending a fortune."

Sara put an ashtray down in front of him "Thanks, Mrs Roberts." Ken took a sip of his drink before continuing,

"Brian, I am disappointed in you, we made a decision, which is in the minutes after being discussed at length.

We went through all the pros and cons then, and we decided on a course of action, now you have gone back on what we have decided. Brian, I cannot work like that, once a thing is agreed upon then let's have action to conclude the matter."

Brian felt that he had been scolded by his school masters, nodding his head he mumbled "Yes, of course Ken, you are right I will see to it first thing in the morning."

"Good, next, have the adverts been placed for production assistant and the extra staff?"

"Yes, they will appear in this week's local paper, we should start getting replies by the end of the week."

"Good," Ken used the word when he had accepted the previous matter as closed and wanted to move onto the next subject. "What about the moving of the machinery?"

He looked at Brian as he said it."That's no problem, as soon as the new tools arrive, we can arrange to have the contractors on the following week, can I ask something?"

It was a sign of the other person's strong personality that Brian felt as if he had to get permission before asking a question.

"Yeah sure, what's that?" he looked up from the notes he was making on a pad.

"Ken, you promised that money would be made available as soon the company had been reconstructed, that was two weeks ago, when can we expect the funds to be made available?"

"By Monday of next week, and before then we will have the confirmation of the signing of the contract"

"That would be handy, the rent is due. and we are under strong pressure from the bank to keep spending down."

"How much is the rent, I've forgotten?" he went back to looking at the notes he had been making. He had spoken briefly as if it did not matter.

Brian thought that was unusual. Ken never seemed to forget anything. even the smallest details he could repeat months later, the thought had crossed his mind even as he was telling him the answer, "Two thousand pounds."

"Not to worry, let me have the demand and I will take care of it." Brian reached into his brief case taking out a file he abstracted a document, "Here, if it's not paid by Friday, they are threatening to take other action."

"We will soon put that right." He said stuffing the paper into his inside pocket.

What Brian did not know at that moment was that Ken was in front of him, and had already approached the Landlords, and discovered it would be only too easy to transfer the leasehold on the property to himself.

He was certain that he only had to make sure the rent was not paid, in the next few days, and then the Landlords would foreclose. It had been agreed with them, for an exchange of money, he would be offered the premises and hence the business with very little outlay, considering its potential worth.

It was a few hours later, although Brian and Sarah felt there was something wrong, they could not in their minds work out what.

After discussing business, the three had relaxed and after a number of drinks their visitor said it was time to go. He got up, and shaking Mrs Roberts hand, left the house in company with Brian, who was to drive him back to the factory where he had left his car.

Winding the window down as Ken drove away, he waved goodbye and then steered in the direction of his own home, musing over events.

At first it had seemed a straightforward assignment, his boss had told him to look at the firms that had applied with tenders for the contract they were offering.

It would have been uncomplicated for his firm to have taken the lowest bidder, but they knew from previous experience that was not always the cheapest way..

When he was first given the assignment, Ken had thought it was a bit of a chore, and not too certain how to go about the task. He decided to see the applicants' premises and at the same time make enquiries through agents on the various firms standing in their sphere.

One or two were obviously out of the running. He was driving home one evening thinking on the day's events, when the thought suddenly struck him how he could involve himself and therefore improve his own earning power.

Not a man to waste time, the following morning he approached his boss and told him what he had in mind, and after a lengthy discussion they reached an agreement, which was satisfactory to both of them.

Later, as the talks got under way with Bar Games Ltd, he started to recognise other possibilities, the main one being that he could very easily take the premises from the present owners without difficulty, by letting them default on the lease.

As he approached his home he was very pleased with himself, it would not take a lot more plotting and planning to have the scheme working, and then he would not only be the majority share holder and a Director of Bar Games, but the lease on the property would be in his name, which without a doubt would put him in a very strong position. Yes indeed, the future did start to look very rosy.

It was a few weeks later and the meeting on a Monday morning in the office of Bar Games, had become a regular occurrence.

The schedule was always the same discussing the events and happenings of the previous week and making plans for the forthcoming one.

They sat in the small office, which was now immaculately tidy, not a speck of dust could be seen anywhere, with the gentle smell of furniture polish pushing the sweeter smell of pipe tobacco into the background.

The trio sat at their usual places, going through papers, checking figures, when Brian broke the silence, "We have had a summons from the Landlords, foreclosing on the lease, I thought you said that you would settle it, Ken?"

"I was going to bring that matter up later in the meeting, we have a small delay."

The husband and wife looked at each other with total surprise on their faces. It was Sarah who spoke "What are you talking about a small delay?"

Ken shrugged his shoulders and looked out of the window as if there was something of interest out there and the question was of no consequence. "There is a delay on the completion of the contract...that's all."

It was Brian's turn to speak "What are you talking about Ken, you said there was no problem and that it would be ready for signing last week, what's the delay now?"

"One of the partners is away at the moment."

"What do you mean? You are not explaining yourself very clearly." Sarah was talking sharply and had leant forward onto the table her eyes blazing.

"You know Barlow, he's a Director really, and it's that funny habit of calling themselves partners that seems to stick..."

There was exasperation in her voice as Sarah said sharply "Would you please explain what you are talking about?"

"I am." Suddenly he felt unsure of himself, he mentally shook himself knowing that if he did not say this right, he could blow the whole deal as it was not too late for them to change their minds. "Barlow has gone away on holiday without signing the contract, there were one or two things he was not happy with and would not sign until they had been ratified."

Brian felt a little sick and knew there was something wrong. He stared his new partner in the eye and he was tapping the desk with his pen when he said sharply "What sort of things need ratifying? And Ken, you did say that there would not be a problem."

Looking from one to the other Ken smiled before he started answering "There is no problem, at least not one that cannot be overcome, a matter of wording which does not really affect us at all, it's just that the document was not typed up before he left and therefore he was not in a position to sign it."

"What about the money?" It was Sarah speaking sharply

"Obviously, that won't be coming until the contracts are signed." Ken was smiling sweetly and had started to wonder when they would get around to the money.

"But Ken, don't you realise without the money we are in all sorts of trouble." Brian had stopped tapping the pen and had put it into his pocket in a fit of frustration.

Looking at the husband and wife with what he hoped passed for the look of innocence on his face, he asked, "What sort of trouble?"

"We have less than ten days to find the rent for the Landlord before he forecloses."

"Surely the Bank will help, they said they would when we went and saw them."

"Ken!" Sarah said sharply. "You are not as naive as that, you know very well that they will only help, if there is a similar investment from our own or another source, so unless that other money is forthcoming then we can forget them."

"I still think they should be approached, and told of the situation, also why not approach the Landlords and tell them the situation and see what they say."

"But Ken, you said you were going to deal with the matter, why didn't you?" Sarah's voice had risen and the anger in her tone was obvious.

"I thought I had made it clear that I could only deal with it when the contracts were complete, and we were in funds."

Sarah had gone red in the face. "You know very well you did not say anything of the sort..." Brian put a restraining hand out, "Now love, don't lose your cool."

"I'm sorry Sarah, I had not meant to mislead you, but I thought you both understood that unless the contracts were signed then there was no money. I thought I had made that clear on a number of occasions."

"No Ken, you did not make that clear..." she spat the words out to him before he interrupted

"If I didn't make it clear than I would have thought it would have been obvious, nobody would put up the sort of money we are talking about without some form of guarantees. What position was you in before I came along, you had been struggling for years waiting for the big break. I am completely disappointed with both your attitudes, I have leant over backwards, and bent the rules to help you...and now you seem to suggest that I have been misleading you." Ken's voice had turned sharp, his attitude cold, as he finished talking, he slammed shut the folder in front of him which he had been working from.

"Ken, nobody is suggesting anything of the sort, it's just that we understood that everything would be all go as from last week."

He had not wanted to mention the word money still feeling a little embarrassed by having to enter into such an agreement after so many years in commerce, although such arrangements were not unusual in business circles, in some way it was still a form of failure.

A small embarrassed silence followed, which Ken did not mind, it suited his purpose. The other two felt that in some way they had offended the one person that had given them so much help in the past few weeks.

Brian did not see the purpose of continuing and said "This is pointless, we are no further forward and I do not see the point in discussing anything further." He stood up saying "I had better deal with matters which are more pressing."

It was a few hours later and both Brian and Sarah felt nauseous with the disappointment and were sitting at home talking over the day's events, "What do you think love?"

"I think we have been misled." She replied looking up from where she had been staring out of the window.

"Yes, I know the feeling, I'm certain he said the money would be available before the contracts were signed."

"Perhaps somebody misled him." she felt defeated and shrugged her shoulder

"Could be, he doesn't seem the sort to make statements that are not true."

"One thing is certain, I doubt if we would have survived if he had not come along."

"But Brian, we had always managed somehow. But now...I just don't know where we are going."

"I'm sure it will turn out just fine, with the new contract and fresh funds, we will be able to get over all our problems."

"And in their place, we will have dear old Ken Williams."

He was reading her mind when he said, "You don't like him very much, do you?"

"Darling, since he's gone back on his word, I don't like him one bit. I don't see how we can trust him again in the future"

Brian was still looking at his wife intently "Try love, we are going to have to work with the man, I'll tell you what we will do, we'll have a party, it's a long time since we had one." He paused before saying." I know we will make it a dinner party,"

Sarah at that moment could not stand the thought of having a gathering in the house saying, "I do not see how that will help but it would be nice, who shall we invite?"

"We can start with Ken, plus one, and we will see who he brings along, and I bet you he's not odd as you are always suggesting."

"Why would we want to invite him plus one as you put it, for...anyway shouldn't we be inviting his boss this mythical man we have never met, which really concerns me – why hasn't he come to see us. Surely, he must be curious, as to who we are?"

Brian responded, "It would be nice to know him in a social atmosphere, and you are right it is about time we met the man who Ken says holds the purse strings, so to speak."

"In that case if it's a party to get to know Ken Williams and his boss, let's go to The Black Rose, that will make six of us, it's their monthly party night shortly we could book a table, I suppose it could be fun." Sarah-s face lit up as she thought of relaxing and perhaps dancing.

"I was thinking of not spending that sort of money that The Black Rose charge, but it would impress his boss … do you know?" He looked a little surprised saying, "We don't even know his name." They sat looking at each other contemplating what they were proposing. Brian said "Is there any reason for not holding it at home?"

."If I'm going to get to know Mr Williams socially, I would prefer to do it when I haven't got to worry about dishes and all the rest of the dinner party mess."

"So be it, I'll put it to Ken in the morning and if it's okay with him and this mythical boss, then I'll organise the seats."

Frances & Lewis

Frances was becoming very fond of Lewis he was kind and gentle with her and after the afternoon when he had made a woman of her they had become very good friends.

It had been the second visit to the venue, and they had once more enjoyed a meal together. She felt very secure with him and was looking forward to being even closer after they left the restaurant.

She had noticed earlier on in the evening that he was dressed differently, where he normally wore a suit with jacket and tie, tonight he was dressed more casually wearing jeans.

Lewis liked Frances and the sex they were enjoying, whilst satisfying, left him feeling a little cheated as the sadist in him demanded more, as he wanted to hurt to get real fulfilment.

In the car going back to her rooms she noticed he was quieter than usual. What she did not know he was struggling with his decision of what he had planned for the rest of the evening.

He could feel the excitement building in him and he knew tonight he was going to have total pleasure and satisfaction.

They arrived back at the safe house and were in her room. Frances was struggling with her outdoor coat, taking it off her shoulders she turned to hang it in the wardrobe.

He was leaning forward against her back putting both his arms around her he took hold of her breasts massaging them through the material of her blouse.

His fingers found the opening and with one quick movement he tore the garment off her. She shouted "Lewis, what are you doing?"

Grabbing her shoulders, he turned her around. Her heart was beating faster and her breasts, covered in a small white bra, were moving in rhythm with her increased breathing.

He was studying them. One of his hands went up and stroked them, before savagely pulling the flimsy material she was wearing, off her. The thin straps attached to the item bruising her as they were ripped from her body.

This was a new Lewis she did not know, and stood looking at him, the white of her breasts prominent which he was teasing.

Although stimulated and she could feel the buzz flowing through her, she was also frightened as he had never acted in this way before.

He was standing close to her and breathing heavily

"Are you going to take that skirt off or shall I do the same with it?"

With shaking hands she reached behind her undoing the clasp, holding it to stop it falling around her ankles, hoping he would calm down before she would have to remove it, however, knowing in her heart he was too worked up, not to go any further.

He started to undo the thick leather belt that held up his trousers.

Fear swept through her, but seeing his under things and the lump between his legs she felt a little easier and felt a growing feeling of desire for him.

If that's all he wanted she would make it easy for him and slipped out of the skirt, standing in front of him in just her pants and stockings.

He had started to free the belt from the eyelets that held it,

"What are you doing that for.?" The fear returning as fast as it had left, and then the thought she had had earlier, of why he was dressed differently tonight, was it significant?

"I told you a few weeks ago that I'm going to teach you a lesson, one you will never forget..."

She had taken the few steps that now separated them, clinging on to him trying to stop him from removing the belt completely.

She tried to kiss him, but he pushed her away. She stumbled over a chair, and before she could right herself, he had pushed her headlong towards the bed.

She cried out more in fear than because he had actually hurt her, she looked at him and saw the smile on his lips, but his eyes were pinpoints and cold as they took in the curves of her body lying on the bed.

"Please Lewis, I did not mean to hurt you." She pleaded as she watched the belt come free and swing through the air making a swishing noise.

She watched in horror as he lowered his brightly coloured boxer shorts his manhood coming clear of its restriction. She cowered back on the bed as far as she could get.

He leant forward and was stroking the belt across her.

The smell of leather was very strong as he slowly caressed her with the strap.

He was like an animal. Frances could see it was of little use struggling he was too strong, and she knew whatever he wanted to do she could not stop him.

She could see it was arousing him sexually as his man hood was growing hard. She had enjoyed it many times, but not like this.

Tears were running down her face. She tried to cover herself with her arms, he dragged them away and not very gently hit her with the belt.

Flipping it across her shoulders and thighs, she felt the stings as it landed.

She looked into his face as she tried to ward off the blows.

They were getting harder, and she could see he was getting pleasure from seeing her discomfort.

He ignored her pleadings and continued to beat her, not too concerned where the strap landed.

She curled herself into a ball trying to protect herself.

Looking at his face she could see he was laughing, and she knew he was enjoying beating her.

Suddenly the blows stopped. She looked up at him. The tears were blurring her vision, her body a mass of aches with pain coming from the worst of the weal's.

She looked at him his legs slightly apart and one hand holding himself. A need to feel him inside her swept through her body.

She had never seen another man naked before Lewis. Although now she had seen it a number of times, she looked in wonderment at its strength.

He was in no hurry leaning over her he grabbed hold of her ankles and pulled her legs towards him.

Somewhere deep inside her she could feel stirrings, she dismissed them and started to struggle she wanted to get off the bed.

She was trying to draw her legs up into a ball and tears were rolling down her face. He slapped her hard and pulled them towards him opening them wide.

"Please don't." She whispered as she glared at him leaning over her – tears were running down her face.

She looked down and was mesmerised by his member waving in front of her.

He took her urgently.

She screamed and then moaned as he continued to satisfy himself.

Her mind was in a whirl, as he grunted, breathing heavily on top of her, so different from previous occasions.

She tried to adjust to this new sensation of hurt and her body being plundered by a man she had started to trust.

Unexpectedly he finished – she lay there with hate in her heart and watched as he gathered his clothing and sat on the bed to get dressed.

She knew somewhere she would get her own back and she allowed the thought to develop in her mind as a way of easing the pain.

He got to the door. "I am looking forward to the next time – in the meantime I'll send the woman up to help you clean up. Now remember, as from tomorrow we will be visiting the venue again so people will get used to seeing us together, and perhaps we can have some fun afterwards."

She sat up with difficulty covering her breasts with her arms, cringing at the thought of meeting this monster again but then how could she avoid it.

Somehow, she knew she would have her revenge. She didn't say anything looking at him defiantly, trying to ignore the pain sweeping through her.

He had only been gone a few minutes when the door opened, and the woman she had come to know as

Rona came into the room, she looked at her curled up on the bed, "I'll get some warm water."

Frances had dozed while she was gone trying not to feel the pain. She saw Rona leaning over the bed, the bowl was balanced on the edge with steam coming from the hot liquid inside.

"You don't look surprised?" She managed to murmur up to her.

"He's done it before." Was the soft reply. "We will soon make you comfortable."

She was surprised at the quiet answer "Who to?"

"To every other girl, that's ever stayed in this room. I knew as soon as I saw you it would only be a matter of time. But funny I thought this time it was different, and he was going to treat you with respect"

Not knowing what to say she looked into her benefactor's face "Really is there something wrong with him - my God, what a sadist."

"You'll be alright in a couple of days, and he hasn't touched your face."

"It hurts just here." Frances said touching her cheek.

"It looks like you'll probably get a bruise there, I'm sorry I didn't see that."

"Has he ever hurt you?"

"No, he won't touch me." She was shaking her head and smiling as she said it.

"Why would you be so different, or does he like them young?"

"He doesn't care too much what they are like - no he won't touch me, I'm his mother."

Frances was shocked, she hadn't thought who the lady was and had not realised there had been any family connection.

She lay back while the elder woman cleaned her and bathed the weal marks.

"He finds it difficult to have a normal relationship with a girl. He wants to hurt them, I've seen him do a lot worse, he has a whip at his home, one poor thing nearly died from the beating he gave her."

"You mean he can do a lot worse, than what he has done to me."

"That's what I'm saying."

"My God, I don't want to see him again, I'd be frightened of what he might do."

"You had better see him as arranged, because they will catch up with you, and punish you badly if you don't go through with the action."

"I hadn't intended to do anything else, anyway we are going straight home from there, by different routes." The thought of the whip went through her mind, "What does he do with this whip."

"I don't know, I've only seen the results, he normally calls me to clear up after him, even if it is at his home." She was rubbing some ointment onto one of Frances sore spots, and then in a sad voice she continued,

"One girl was still tied up when I got there, I think that's what he does, she was very ill, he wouldn't say much about it, only that she had tried to fight him."

"Don't you say anything to him?"

She shrugged her shoulders "I used to, but it doesn't do any good, that's the way he is."

"Why don't you tell the police?"

The older woman stopped and looked her in the eyes, "What do you mean."? Her voice had gone hard.

"I didn't mean actually tell the police, what I meant was threaten to tell the authorities." She modified the word police, having seen the reaction on the other persons face.

And what do you think he would do to me, if I was to do that?"

"You said he would not hurt you, you said you were his mother."

"If he was to feel threatened, there is no telling what he would do, mother or not. I told you what he did to that other poor lass, you should have seen her tied hand and foot, and barely alive. It's lucky I'm a trained nurse."

Frances did not know what to say, but she was frightened, she would have to see him before the day of the operation, she was frightened he would start hitting her again, and the thought of being whipped, sent a cold chill up her spine.

The following few days passed in horror of the front door opening and hearing him enter the house. The feeling which had been building in her she had thought was love but she now realised it had only been the unique attraction of a male friend and now that had turned to hate.

She watched the bruise on her face develop, and grow darker, she studied the mirror and watched as the swelling went down and wondered how she was going to face him again, without collapsing in fright.

The Saturday was cold and bright. Frances, woke up feeling better than she had the day before, she still felt sore, but the stinging had gone, it was a little while later that she first felt ill, she had to rush to the toilet where she was violently sick.

Returning to the bedroom feeling very weak, she started to wonder what new horrors were waiting for her, didn't pregnant women get sick in the morning?

She did not understand pregnancies, she had never been taught anything about it and did not know if she could be with child after the few couplings she had had with Lewis.

Her strong Catholic upbringing had not taught her anything about contraception or prevention. She knew nothing about any device and he certainly hadn't taken any form of precautions, she only expected it could have happened.

She sat on the bed and started to cry, she felt as if in the past few days she had cried all the tears she had, but the depression was now complete, she felt so low, her world was in tatters and now this final blow. She tried to reason with herself, but it was no good, she was certain she was with child, that monster's child.

She lay on her bed most of the morning planning and scheming how to get her revenge.

~~~

In South London the arrangements were now complete to be able to deliver the bombs to The Black Rose and they were loaded into a Ford Transit Van.

~~~

Jane

Jane Chariton was only three years old when her father died, and she could still recall the hurt of remembering her mother crying every night after the tragic accident.

Now, fifteen years later they were very close, and people often mistook them for sisters, much to the pleasure of Ivy, her mother.

After Dad died, and the loss of his weekly wage, the family's income hardly met their day to day needs.

She had had the choice when she was fifteen either to continue her schooling or to look for a job.

It was to help the family's finances that she opted to abandon her education, although her mother had not wanted her to do that, as she felt her scholarship would be a better option, as no doubt she would need the use of her learning later in life..

She had excitedly joined a local firm of tool makers, as a trainee in the offices with the promise that they would teach her how to type.

Jane had been there for less than a year when, what had been a busy office, the workload got less.

So after only being at the firm for ten months she was made redundant leaving her to join the unemployed queue, as it was too late to take the schooling option.

She had been very miserable about the whole episode especially as most of her friends were still at school, which meant being bored all day waiting for school to finish.

Jane spent many fruitless months looking for work, always with the same answers, either not enough experience or her qualifications were not good enough.

Not being an idle girl, she had become desperate and depressed about her situation, daily going through the ritual of job hunting.

Every morning she would be at the newsagents waiting for the first daily papers to arrive, and then she would promptly search the columns looking for a vacancy that would suit her experience and qualification.

Jane became very friendly with the newspaper seller, Bernard Walters, who knew of her plight and marvelled at the way she stuck to the task of finding a job.

Then one morning he had some good news for her, but to his surprise and disappointment she did not turn up as usual. He could not understand her absence and found himself worrying about her welfare and considered if she was ill.

He had also missed the slim cheeky faced blond. As he knew where there was a vacancy and he knew she would be prepared to consider anything, during his lunch break he went to her house.

At first Bernard felt a bit foolish as the door was not answered immediately and started thinking to himself what right did he have to be there ... perhaps she had already found work and had started that morning.

Nevertheless, he waited, and was about to go when he heard movement inside the house.

It was a long time before the front door was answered and peeping around it stood a long pink dressing gown, a tousle of blond hair on top with a tissue on the end of one arm.

She did not recognise him until he spoke with his normal greeting. "Oh, hi." She replied wondering why he had come round.

"I missed you in the shop this morning. Now I can see why you did not turn up."

"Yes, I'm not feeling very well....I would not want you catching it so I won't invite you in." She continued standing at the door although she did not feel like it, she was trying to smile.

"Thank you, but I can't stop, it's just that I have some news for you and it can't wait." Jane brightened up immediately, "Do you mean about a job?"

"Yes...that's right, it's not much but the pay's not bad, the downside is it is odd hours."

"Oh, thank you, thank you, odd hours does not matter, please stop teasing and tell me where."

"I was having my normal drink last night, and the Landlord said he was looking for someone full time. I immediately thought of you and I told him that I knew just the person. I also told him how efficient and diligent you were."

He was smiling at her and then said, "I hope you are pleased, he would like to see you and asked if you could manage this lunchtime?"

"Super, that's really super, thank you so much I am feeling quite excited and feeling much better.

Where is it, the pub I mean?" She was beaming and the thrill of starting work again was driving the aches and pains away.

It was his turn to feel thrilled not only because he had done the right thing but seeing the change in her was in itself rewarding, with a big grin he said.

"Burt the Landlord at The Black Rose, it's that big place that lies back off the road with a large car park in the front, if you go in and ask for him, he is expecting you."

"I know where you mean and thank you so much, but I am going to miss seeing you in the morning." He was nodding his head "Yes, so am I, perhaps when you are settled in your new job, we can see each other?"

"Thank you, I would like that very much and anyway if you go to this pub to drink then maybe I will see you there."

Abruptly she realised what a mess she must look, she ran her fingers through her hair in an attempt to tidy herself "I had better hurry if I'm going to make it in time."

"Yes, I had better let you get on, bye for now." He was smiling as he turned away.

That had been seven months earlier, and now although she liked working at The Black Rose, she still looked for another occupation, something where the hours were not so staggered. As she normally did not start work until late in the morning, she still managed to see Bernard in the paper shop on the way to The Black Rose.

Ivy, her mother, still worked, although only part time in a shop, where she had started after the loss of her husband. She was proud and especially close to her daughter, they both enjoyed each other's companionship, which also meant they could discuss matters together.

She was so completely wrapped up in her offspring that she had no other real friends, her whole life was evolved in what her daughter was doing.

Ivy had got used to her lifestyle, and the thought of going out did not occur to her, as she never thought about it. On occasions the pair would visit shops, but they were close in each other's company and enjoying their home life, to have a need for socialising.

Normally Jane, would arrive home at about eleven thirty in the evening, Ivy would be waiting for her, and would quickly put on something hot for her to drink. Jane would sit down and happily chat away about the day's events.

It was coming up to Mrs Chariton's birthday, and Jane was sitting in her usual chair looking a little serious.

"What's the matter love you look a bit down?" Ivy had put the book down she was reading to look up at her daughter.

"Nothing really Mum, I was thinking it's your birthday on Saturday."

"Yes, what about it dear? Now I do not want any fuss, I have had plenty in the past and I know what they are like."

"Alright Mum, I know, but this time I just thought that we should do something special."

"We never have done that before, you know, and as I just said, I don't like a fuss."

"I know Mum, but just this once, it would be nice, and it would be different and it is a special birthday and I would like us to celebrate it."

Ivy got up from her chair and was making her way out of the room. "I am quite happy, maybe we will have a small celebration here."

Jane had followed her mother into the kitchen. "There is a party coming up at the pub, and I thought as it is your birthday you might like to come along. It will be a great evening."

"I don't know, love...do you want your drink here or in the lounge?" Not waiting for an answer, Ivy returned to where they normally sat in the evening.

Jane again followed her mother into the other room as she continued to talk, "It's always a good evening, some of the officers come over from the Army barracks, and there is a cabaret, and if you want a meal then the Governor said he would give us a discount."

"It all sounds grand, but I don't know if I would enjoy myself, I never have been to anything like that before, why don't we sleep on it and see."

"If you are going to come, I need to book the table. Also, this evening will be more special, as the new manager will be there, who is taking over next week, when Burt leaves."

"Oh, that is a shame, as I know you like the Landlord and his missus." She thought for a moment "Anyway darling, I wouldn't have anyone to go with, and what would I wear?

Mum! You have got plenty of things to wear, and Pam's parents will be there, and you could sit with them, they are great fun. Also, I would like to invite Bernard from the paper shop to join us."

"I hardly know them! I've only met them the once and that was last Christmas. Oh, I don't know, and your friend from the paper shop, I don't think I have ever said hello to him, let alone spend the evening in his company."

"You have got to come Mum, anyway you have met Bernard before because he came around here last Christmas and you said he was ever so nice."

Jane stood with her hands on her hips looking down at Ivy who had sat down. "We never do anything on your birthday, and the Governor will let me sit with you for a while, while the cabaret is on." She walked around feeling exasperated and sat down in an armchair opposite her mother.

Mrs Chariton felt pleased and excited about being asked, but she was not used to going out in company and was frightened that she would make a fool of herself. She had a mental fight trying to make up her mind, and because her daughter was so happy about her going, she decided not to disappoint her.

"Alright love, I'll go but I don't want to be too late."

Jane leant over and flung her arms about her mother kissing her, "Mum, I just know we are going to have a fabulous evening."

~~~

In the South London a plan had been formed of how to get the bombs into The Black Rose.

~~~

Bill & Bobby

Bill Perdwey was suffering, it had been his wedding anniversary the day before, and he and his wife had gone out to celebrate with a few of their friends.

It was six thirty in the morning as he hauled himself up into the cab of the lorry, the thought crossed his mind that late night drinks and early mornings did not agree with him.

He was checking the documents of the vehicle and noting the mileage and writing it into the log. He looked across to his mate saying, "My mouth feels like Blackwall Tunnel on a damp foggy night."

is assistant, who had worked with him for over two years, grinned back at him. "Good night last night then?"

"Bloody good...you should have seen my missus doing the Can – Can, all went well until she tried to do the dance on the tabletop - what a 'to do!' There was the manager of the restaurant, a tall skinny guy, trying to get her down, and then over went the table, with the missus landing in some guys lap, and of course his chair went over...laugh."

His friend was laughing "What happened then, Bill?"

Bill was busy altering the seat, so it was comfortable on the big Leyland dray wagon, he wound the window down and adjusted the mirrors on the door, nodding to his mate to do the same on his side of the vehicle.

"All hell breaks loose, and there is the stupid bloody manager standing there saying, 'there ain't no dancing here – it's not allowed.' You can imagine the roar that went up with that statement."

Bobby, the assistant, who had been stowing the lunch boxes and thermos flask on the shelf behind the seat, was chuckling "Were the Old Bill called?"

"No, he didn't have that sort of bottle. No, the missus gets up from the floor, because its where she finishes up – she got her skirt round her neck, she didn't half look a pretty sight."

The other was looking at him wide eyed "Did you say anything to her?"

"You got to be joking, have you tried saying anything to my missus she'd give you a verbal bashing, and you would be sorry you said anything."

Bill had been cleaning the windscreen and passed the leather over to Bobby to clean the other side. "I've only met her once, and that was at last year's firms do, nice lady, likes her fun."

"Come on let's stop this chit chat and get this thing on the road." He turned the ignition key of the big diesel engine which shuddered, coughed and then started rumbling sending clouds of blue smoke out of the exhaust. "Did you pick the papers up?"

"Yes Bill, as usual, and you are going to love this – it's the Guildford run." He was grinning at the driver.

"Oh bloody hell, not all that way in this crab of a lorry - that would be our luck today, and me feeling like a dead horse. If we don't get going, we won't have time to stop at Lilly's, for breakfast."

The huge lorry with its keg barrels and crates of beer secured on the back turned slowly out of the gates of the Brewery, the engine gathering more power as it warmed up.

Bill was expertly wheeling it on to the road his hands automatically going across the controls of the vehicle and saying to his mate "it is about time you learned to drive." Looking at his watch he added "We will just have time for breakfast but we will have to be quick."

At their normal morning stop two burly men stood in the queue waiting to be served at the counter, both were dressed, as others the patrons in Lilly's road side cafe, in jeans and a coloured shirt most wearing a duffle type coat.

The tall one, a broad shouldered individual, while the other, called Eddie, was the opposite and was fidgety and frequently glancing at the door – he leant over to whisper to his colleague "Why do you think they are late." He looked up at the clock on the wall and repeated himself "Why do you think they are late, do you think they are coming?"

"Will you shut up relax and move along you are holding the queue up."

Looking out through the grubby windows at the car park he continued "What do you think is keeping them?"

is colleague turned around sharply "How the hell would I know – stop worrying they will be here, if not we know where they are going and we will find them on the road."

Nothing more was said, although the smaller of the two constantly turned to look out at the wide open space in front of the property, where the lorries waited.

The pair collected their food they had ordered and sat down at a table, and quickly tucking into the hot breakfast.

"Looking at that door won't make them come any quicker, and also people are starting to notice." It had been said with a mouthful of food as if the words did not matter.

The second of the two was obviously nervous his fingers were twitching "Well then, what do you think is keeping them?"

"God man, if you ask that one more time I'm going to throw you out of here on your bleeding ear; anyway you can stop worrying, they have just pulled into the car park."

"Where?" He had started to look over his shoulder.

"Don't turn round." He replied sharply "I can see them."

Bobby and Bill pushed the door open and strode into the premises, the entrance way thudded shut behind them as they walked over to the counter.

Lil looked up at them "You are a little later than other times. Is it the usual for breakfast?"

Bobby punched his mate in a friendly gesture on the arm "He had problems getting out of his pit this morning, too much booze the night before, and now they are sending us on the worst and longest run out to Guildford."

"Serves you right Bill - find a table and I'll bring it over for you."

While waiting for the food, Bill took a mouthful of hot strong tea saying with a big smile on his face "That is more than welcome."

The food arrived and they both started to eat and Bobby could not help noticing the pair of men, one of whom would quickly look away when he saw they had been spotted by the new arrivals.

After hurriedly eating their breakfast the two Dray men got up, and after a chat with some of the other regulars, they went out to the wagon. Both walked around it checking on the load to see if it was secure. A few minutes later they were driving out of the lorry park.

In the cafe the tall one was saying "Sit down, we do not need to leave as yet." He had put a restraining hand on the others arm.

"But we will lose sight of them..." he was sitting down slowly.

"Shut up, people are starting to take notice." He had lowered his voice "We know where they are going so today it's not going to be difficult to catch up with them." He winked at his companion who had settled down, although he still had a nervous twitch.

It was over two hours later before Bill realised that they were being followed, as he had frequently noticed the small van in his mirrors.

At first, he didn't say anything to Bobby. He drove along getting more and more angry, and the longer they were behind him, the more short tempered he got. In the end Bobby had to say something.

'"What the bloody hells the matter with you, I know you have had a late night, but you don't have to take it out on me with that bloody long face, do you?"

"Sorry Son, the bloody Brewery are spying on us." As he said it, he checked in his mirror to see if the van was still behind.

"What the bloody hell would they want to do that for?" Bobby often used that phrase as he leant forward so he could see through the mirror on his side of the lorry. "Blimey that looks like a van which was parked in Lilly's."

"So they have been with us all that time." He paused not understanding why they were being followed.

Bobby asked if he knew why the Brewery would have an interest in them. "How would I know why they are following us? I'll have something to say about it when we get back."

"I thought they only spied on people who they thought had been on the fiddle." Bobby was looking at his mate.

"Exactly, we had better be on our toes, and do everything by the book." He glanced at his mate wondering if he had done something which the Brewery was not pleased with.

"You're not on the take, are you Bill?" Not waiting for an answer he continued, "Because if you are I'm not getting any"

Bill looked sharply at his friend "I don't know what you are talking about and you don't have to worry Son - of course I'm not, anyway if I was I would include you. Wouldn't I?

"I don't know, do I? But tell me why they are following us?"

The driver shrugged his shoulders. They drove on in silence both feeling a little uncomfortable, then Bill said "I can assure you Bobby I have not been on the take, and as I said, if I had I would have involved you."

Bobby chose not to answer trying to work out in his mind if at any time he had been suspicious of any transaction Bill had made.

"Now don't you go sulking on me – anyway, if we don't get a move on, we won't get to Guildford before The Black Rose closes, and you know how they hate that."

They drove on in silence before Bill said "I don't know why they provide us with this old banger of a lorry to go all the bloody way to Guildford, there are more modern vehicles - very shortly we have got the long drag up the hill to the Hogs Back and we will waste more time."

Bobby had sat in silence for some time before saying "Well, what am I to think? We got the Brewery on our back and they would only do that if there was something wrong."

"Leave it out, Son – how many more times have I got to tell you, I have done nothing wrong, anyway how could I, you have got the tickets."

"Yeah, I know all that and I'm wondering how you have done it."

Bill changed down a gear for the start of the hill. "I've just told you, I haven't done anything. Hang about they are catching us up."

"I wonder what they want?" Bobby was talking more to himself, his voice hardly audible over the noise of the engine, as the big dray lorry started the climb up the steep hill.

Bill ignored the statement, although he was trying to work out the answer himself, and then it suddenly occurred to him that as he was not on the take and cheating their employers, then it could only be Bobby.

He glanced at his companion who was looking out the side window, watching the fields going past. Bill put the thought out of his mind, it just was not possible.

Not many words had been exchanged between the two men in the small van, as it had followed the dray on its various deliveries through the suburbs of London.

"Where do you want to stop them, Shaun?"

"I'll tell you where. The important thing is to keep close to them."

"It must be pretty obvious to them that we are following them."

"Yeah, but don't worry about it."

The lorry was crawling up a long incline, the van a few yards behind. Shaun looked across at Eddie who was driving,

"Okay, near the top of this hill there is an off the road lay by in some trees, pull up alongside them so I can tell them to stop there. Now you know what you have got to do, just take the kid, and I'll meet you later where we arranged."

"Who's worrying now?"

There something to worry about now, just be certain you get your end right."

PERCY W. CHATTEY

Eddie changed gear and pulled the van out to come alongside the lorry.

Bill was watching them and saw the movement. He glanced across at Bobby, "Here we go, they are coming alongside us now."

"What the hell do they want in the middle of nowhere, Bill I don't like this one bit."

"It certainly seems strange, they are waving for us to stop in that lay by, aren't they going to get a shock when they start checking."

Bill drove off the main road into the recreation Area of the lay by. He pulled the handbrake on hard, switching off the engine in the same movement.

By this time the two men were standing each side of the cab, Eddie the smaller of the two was next to Bobby.

Shaun opened the cab door, "Driver, your assistant is to get down and you are to move over into his seat."

Bobby heaved himself out of the cab without a thought, and to his surprise Shaun was climbing into the driver's seat encouraging Bill to move over.

Bill looked at his new companion in the vehicle wondering what was going on. He didn't like the look on the fellows face and said his thoughts, "What the bloody hell is going on?" he took a sheet off the rear shelf and pointed to it "Look here, I signed for this heap of a lorry, if you are going to drive it then bloody well sign here."

"All you have got to do is shut up, and listen, and then no one gets hurt."

"What are you talking about, if we don't get a move on we are going to miss the delivery and then there will be hell to play?"

Shaun drew a pistol from under his coat, holding it so Bill could see the barrel "Your friend has one pointing at his head, now stay still and shut up."

Eddie had edged back giving Bobby plenty of room, "Now give me a hand to get two barrels out of the van. Remember get this wrong and your friend's a dead man."

With the terrorist watching he unloaded the beer cask from the rear of the van, and with difficulty heaved them on to a vacant spot on the back of the flat body of the dray, all the time his mind was racing trying to find an answer to what was obviously a dangerous situation,

He tried to look at Bill to see if he could get some form of lead, to no avail, the reflection on the cab windows made it difficult to look into it, and in any case he couldn't see how his partner could possibly convey anything to him, they were being too closely watched.

He wasn't certain when it first occurred to him, it had certainly been lurking in his mind, but it suddenly was very clear, that whatever these people were up to they couldn't let him and his driver go free to tell everyone.

The fear gripped his stomach, his mouth went dry. He looked at the second keg now sitting on the back of the lorry, mocking him in his foolishness for not putting up more resistance. But then, what could he have done?

"Good, now I want you to get in the back of the van." Eddie was waving a revolver in the direction he wanted him to take.

Bobby looked at the van parked in front of the lorry with its two rear doors wide open. "What for?"

"Don't fuck around with me and do as you're told and get in the van."He was threatening him with the gun again.

Bobby was feeling defiant, the initial shock was wearing off, and now he wanted to fight. "What you going to do, shoot us out here on the main road?"

"If necessary, stop arguing and get into the van."

Bobby was backing away trying to put as much distance as possible between him and the other man, in the hope he could break for the small wood that lay to one side of the road.

The terrorist sensed what was in his mind and moved closer to him, raising his voice."Do as you're bloody told, and move over towards the van."

Bobby realised he needed to do something, he was too close to him to just start running, he moved towards the small vehicle the other followed, he grabbed hold of the open door and slammed it into the others face.

Without another thought Bobby turned and ran, his feet slipped on the steep muddy banking to the side of the lay by.

He could hear the shout of "Come back." He took no notice, making a grab for the giant bush that grew just off the roadside.

He could hear shouting behind him, but he kept going. The door to the cab of the lorry opened, and he heard the deeper voice of the other man.

He threw himself at the small wire fencing, his heart beating wildly, his back feeling very exposed to the two men, waiting for them to shoot.

In the cab of the lorry, Bill, who had been sitting wondering what action he could take, trying to work out a way to disarm the thug sitting holding a pistol at him, saw Bobby take off for the undergrowth.

For a small period of time, his captor was looking elsewhere, following what was happening outside.

Bill made a grab for the gun, at the same time the terrorist turned and opened the door to the cab.

The small chance had gone, but to his relief the terrorist was getting out.

Without wasting time Bill crossed over and got into the driver's seat and pressed the starter button and in the same movement threw it into gear.

The big engine still hot from use, picked up immediately, he let the clutch out and leaning over the steering wheel he started to turn it to bring the vehicle around the parked van.

There was a deafening roar.

The window beside Bill's head shattered into small pieces, the bullet disappearing across the road.

The shock made Bill stall the engine, and he turned and looked with horror at the gunmen, who was standing outside the vehicle, he had opened the door and looking through the opening.

The gun went off a second time, the energy of the bullet pushed him across the cabin, his body slipped forward, his eyes staring through the windscreen.

Bobby, on hearing the shots had never known such fear and ran all the faster.

The ground was extremely uneven, and he was going as fast as he could aiming for the row of trees in the distance, tripping across the undergrowth sliding on the soft ground that was wet with the constant rain.

There was further shouting behind him, which added additional energy to his pumping legs, he slipped again and fell headlong onto the ground.

In a running crouch he came off the earth trying to put as much distance in the shortest possible time and wondering what had happened to his partner.

All the time Bobby was waiting for the shot that would bring him down.

He could feel the fear, taste it almost.

He wanted to be sick, his heart felt as if it would burst, he could hear it pounding in his ears.

His breath was coming in short sharp puffs, his hands trembling, his legs shaking and going weak, making it difficult to run.

How could this be happening, he could hear the odd vehicle on the main road, and yet here he was running for his life.

He heard the sharp report of the gun, the shock wave followed immediately, earth kicked up in front of him.

Bobby stumbled, trying to regain his balance by pushing along with his hands.

Sweat was starting to run into his eyes. He tried to push it away, he was so near to the edge of the wood, which way should he go.

He tried to look about him to get his bearing to see where to hide.

His eyes wouldn't focus, everything was swimming in a red haze, he looked sharply over his shoulder, he saw one raising his gun.

He threw himself to the left, trying to get away. Once more he heard the gun go off, once more he felt the shock wave, and once more he knew it had missed.

As he got to the very edge of the wood, in his haste he did not see the old barbed wire fence, which had many years ago collapsed as the posts holding it had rotted away.

He didn't see the entanglement of rusty wire still attached to the pole, but now lay hidden by the undergrowth.

The pain in his leg as a barb dug deeply into his calf as he rushed past, was his first awareness.

He stopped and looked down, cursing himself when he saw how he was impaled, he tried to untangle himself, panic seizing him.

He never heard the shot that killed him, the bullet knocking him flat, the wire entangled around his feet and ankles.

The two gunmen stood looking down at his body, the younger of the two was white and shaking slightly.

Shaun looked at him, "Is it your first?" He nodded his head, "What are we going to do with him?"

"Leave him, we'll get some branches and cover him up, get some tools out of the van and cut some from that bush over there, make sure you hide him good. Oh, and take any identification off him, we don't want him being traced too soon."

What'll you do?" Eddie was looking white and standing rigid.

"I'll tidy up the lorry it would be best if we left them both here and hide the van elsewhere."

Neither of them moved for a few minutes, suddenly the elder of the two said, "Come on, get a move on, otherwise we will be here all day."

Detective Inspector Green

The Police Station for the area in Woodbridge Road, Guildford, was in an early Georgian, square shaped building.

To the rear was the Section House, converted from what were the stables in the original property and where the young trainee Police Cadets lived.

The main part of the building to the front, was where the Uniformed Officers worked.

To one side and out of direct reach from the public was the CID (Criminal Investigation Division) Offices, and Detective Inspector Green had his office.

He had just returned from a meeting with senior personnel and others more senior to his rank, where they had discussed the recent attacks by terrorists on Public Houses.

On two occasions the perpetrators had parked a car to the front of the establishment and detonated explosives, destroying the front of two of the public houses, killing and maiming the revellers inside the bar.

His telephone rang while he was pondering over the details, he had learned that day.

"Detective Inspector the front desk here, we have some serious trouble at the Rodborough Building can you attend?"

The problem of working out what Public Houses maybe at risk, on what he thought of as his patch, would have to wait, until this new problem was out of the way.

When he arrived at the site of the disturbance the difficulty had been resolved and he was not needed.

Detailing one of the younger Detectives to go with him, he decided there was no better time than the present to start a tour of the Public Houses, to spread the word to be on their guard against a repeat of what had occurred at other establishments.

Fifteen minutes later he arrived at The Black Rose.

The Black Rose

Burt was serving in the public bar and was frequently looking at the dark brown wall clock, which he knew was ten minutes fast, set that way so as to fool the customers as to the actual time.

Looking away from it and continuing his normal task, at this time of day, of cleaning glasses in an automatic way, and loading them neatly in rows on to a shelf.

As he did so he shouted, "Time gentlemen." It had been a busy lunch hour and a few of the usual late drinkers were playing darts, with others standing in groups talking.

Irene came around from the saloon, "The draymen haven't been yet, Burt?" It was more of a question than a statement.

"Yes, I know - I wish they would get here earlier, it's almost closing time, I think I will have to have a word with the Brewery." Burt was stacking the last of the glasses.

"Perhaps they have left us off the list and are not coming?" she had leant on a bench seat under the window to look outside saying "there is no sign of them."

"I know they have done it before, but it had better not be today otherwise we will not have enough beer for this weekend?" Burt had looked across at his wife.

She responded by saying "It is getting very late I don't mind staying open for a little while longer if we know they are coming. You could go then and have your rest."

"Thank you, but as you say we will wait a little longer, if you are worried about it love, why not phone the Brewery ... I better get on, there are still some things to do."

"No Burt, you phone them, I'm never certain who to speak to?"

"God woman, a simple phone call, is it that difficult? I'll do it in a moment." He had looked at her in exasperation.

The short exchange of words left an atmosphere with other people looking at each other.

One of the fellows standing at the bar gave a short laugh, someone else started to tell a joke, slowly the usual friendly warmth returned.

Irene had disappeared, leaving Burt to wonder about his beer delivery, he looked at the clock speculating if he should phone or not. And then he put the whole question out of his mind and got on with serving the last drinks before they closed.

It was ten minutes later that he poked his head round the saloon bar, "I've had a nag at the Brewery, its Bill Perdway and Bobby that are on the way to us, they are surprised that they have not arrived by now, so they should be here shortly."

Without waiting for a reply, he returned to the public bar annoyed with himself for letting his impatience get the better of him.

~~~

The two Irishmen had returned to the vehicles, Eddie was asking "What shall we do with the van?"

"You drive it and I will be right behind you in the lorry. We need to park the van up because we will need it later. As you go into the town there is a car park on the right hand side leave it there and then come and join me in the lorry."

He looked at his watch "It is getting a bit late and I am told he will close up if we are not there sharp."

Eddie, had parked the van as planned and was now back in the dray. He was busy looking through the clip board that he had found in the cab and was trying to work out the paper work.

"I hope you know what you are doing." Shaun was talking to Eddie. "I thought you were supposed to know about the delivery side."

"I do, it's just that they seemed to have changed it since I worked there. There seems to be another sheet which wasn't there before. Never mind you get on with the driving, I'll work it out and don't worry it'll be alright."

"Look man, I hope you know what you are doing, they must not expect anything unusual when we get to the pub."

There was tension in the cab between the two men knowing everything could go wrong if the Landlord was suspicious and checked the load. "Hurry up we are coming up to the pub now."

Nothing was said as they turned into the car park and Shaun pulled the truck up outside the public bar, "Eddie, see where they want us to be, and remember when we start unloading, for Christ sake don't drop those two barrels down the cellar, we will have to lower them down."

Eddie grunted, swinging his legs from the vehicle and jumping down he made his way to the bar, and saw Burt who looked up in surprise. "Eh governor, where do you want us?"'

Burt was surprised to see the strange drayman as he was fond of Bill Perdway and was looking forward to a little chat with him "Where's the two regulars?"

On a different route today, I would think, we are still trying to find our way about, that's why we are a bit late."

He put the board with the delivery sheets clipped to it on the bar holding a pen out indicating he wanted Burt to sign, he did not know if it was true, although it sounded right when he said. "It's your normal load and just as you ordered. Where shall we put it?"

"Hold on, I'll show you." Burt lifted the flap and came from behind the bar, "Do you want a hand? You'll be done that much quicker."

"No thanks mate, my driver is a strict Union Man, he'd call the bleeding lot of us out on strike if you were to do that."

"Just as you please." They walked around the side of the building waving for the dray to follow. "That's funny really, I phoned your office about half an hour ago to see where you were, and they said it was the regular crew."

"Probably didn't want to upset you, or as I suspect they don't know what's happening in that office."

Burt had taken some keys from his pocket and was starting to unlock a door; "This it then?" Eddie was looking around him as he said it.

"Yes, you'll find the trap door over there, I'll unlock it from the inside."

Burt returned to the bar, to help clear away after the lunch time session, leaving the two bogus draymen to unload.

The first two barrels, were unloaded with care, gently taken from the back of the lorry, and with the help of ropes, lowered into the cellar.

Eddie took from his pocket a sheet of paper, opening it out on a crate of beer, he looked down on a plan of the cellar complex.

Turning his head towards Shaun he said, "When I first saw these drawings I thought it was a very considerable area but now I'm here it looks even bigger."

"Alright, never mind about that, just tell me where they have got to go."

Eddie studied the document a little longer saying, "While I work out where the two items should be, why don't you go back to the lorry and get the sign and bring it down here."

He went back to the drawing turning it one way, then another so as to get his bearings.

Finally, when Shaun returned, he pointed his finger to the sheet of paper saying, "I think we are standing here."

"Look Eddie, I don't want you to think about us standing somewhere, I want you to be certain." Shaun was looking concerned. "Now where have I got to put these things?"

"Look here, over there is the step and the hatch where we have brought the beer in, so that means they have got to be the other side of that arch.

It looks like there are two places where they pump the beer to the bars, one from this side, and there is another as I just said from the other side of that archway."

"Come on let's do it otherwise the governor is going to start wondering what we are up to."

A few minutes later they moved the two bombs to where they had planned for them to be and hung a sign on them saying 'For Backup Only.'

~~~

Mrs Perdway turned over in bed as she heard her husband get up. Her head was thumping, however she managed, to squint at the illuminated figures on the digital clock, sighed as she saw the time and closed her eyes and went back to sleep.

Finally, the same time piece told her it was time to get up otherwise she would be late arriving at work for her part time job.

Dragging herself out of bed she was not certain how to face the day as she was not feeling very well, with a very bad hangover from the previous evening activities.

Ultimately after some strong sweet tea she found the energy to leave the house.

She was feeling delicate all that day and somehow managed to complete afficiently her hours reassembly items she was working on and was not sorry when it was time to go home.

As soon as she arrived home in the early afternoon, she lay on the bed and had a sleep, which was unusual for her, but after the late night she felt in need of it.

Afterwards she visited her married daughter, who lived within walking distance, played with her first and only grandchild, who was nearly two, before returning home to get Bill's dinner ready.

She had made toad in the hole, which was cooking nicely in the oven and should be ready for her husband, when he normally got home, just after six.

The early evening dragged on, the meal had been ready for a long time but still no sign of Bill, not unusual for him to be late but he normally telephoned if he was going to be.

At a quarter to eight she could stand it no longer, picking the telephone up and dialled the Brewery.

"I'm sorry Mrs Perdway, we haven't seen him or his mate either, in fact we are waiting for him to return so we can close the office."

"Are you telling me they have not come back from their deliveries?"

"Yes, that is what I am saying, I can't understand where they can possibly be, perhaps the lorry has broken down, I wouldn't worry he's got to be somewhere. Let me have your number and as soon as we have heard from him, I'll call you back."

Despite the reassurance she was a little worried, so she turned the evening meal out, which by now was just about ruined, and waited for the phone to ring.

When it finally did the mystery of her missing husband deepened, she was told that all the deliveries for that day had been completed, but where they had gone from there no one knew.

The girl in the office continued to say as soon as they heard from them, they would telephone and let her know.

What nobody knew, at that time, was the lorry was left in a lorry-park on the outskirts of London, where it would be found three days later.

Liz & Christopher

Christopher Perkins had finally taken the plunge and told his wife about his newfound love, and that he planned to leave home and live with her.

or weeks he had been trying to pick an argument so that he could leave in a rage, but it was difficult to provoke his wife into a disagreement, as she would agree with everything he said, which whilst frustrating was difficult to get really worked up about.

The day that Liz found the flat, which was nicely furnished and situated in a very pleasant neighbourhood, he knew he could not put off the day any longer, and that he would have to tell his wife of his intentions.

He was equally surprised by her reaction, she calmly told him she was pleased for him, and that she had been thinking of leaving him for some time, as she was fed up with the South of England and that she would prefer to take the children, and go and live with her parents in the North.

It was not until later did he realise that nothing had been said about their marriage, and whether they should get a divorce.

The separation was dealt with as if she was going on holiday, and a little while later he found himself with an empty house and a girl friend with a brand new flat.

Liz insisted that they should live in the flat until the ownership of the house had been settled; she also made it clear that if they were going to live in the house then it would have to be redecorated from top to bottom.

And so Chris and Liz, settled in together, not much of a surprise to everyone in the bank, and of course there were those amongst the staff who said they had known all along, but had not wanted to say anything, which everyone thought unusual. '

The sheer bliss of living with Liz made Christopher's head swim, she was so different from his wife in every way, she always dressed nicely, even when cooking breakfast she looked smart and he marvelled at the way she achieved this with the minimum of fuss.

The future was looking good for them, his wife had written and said that if he wanted to sell the house they would split the proceeds, or he could pay her half the value, and that she had seen a solicitor to arrange a divorce.

It was Saturday morning and Liz was first out of bed, she looked out of the window and laughingly said." Guess what, it's still raining."

He turned over and grunted, opening two bleary eyes looking at the beauty of her naked back.

She turned, "Come on dozy, up you get, breakfast will be ready in ten minutes."

He made a grab for her, she stepped back out of his way, he sprawled across the floor, she laughed running from the room.

After breakfast the dark clouds left the sky and the sun swamped the outside in dazzling light.

Christopher was not looking forward to the afternoon as it would be the day, he met her mother and father.

Before that chore, there was a need to sell his previous home, as he could not raise enough money to pay his wife for her half. With that in mind they went to the High Street, where he knew of an Estate Agent who he had met through his position in the bank.

They reached The Black Rose, quite late in the afternoon after the Pub had closed from the lunchtime session.

He was still feeling exceptionally nervous about meeting her parents for the first time. Liz was very happy that everything was working out just nicely.

Burt opened the door to their knocking, "Hi Dad, why don't you get a bell fixed on this door?"

"What" And have every kid in the neighbourhood ringing it...Hello this must be Chris? How do you do, I'm Dad."

Chris instantly warmed to her father and before either of them could say any more he continued, "Come on up and meet mother, she's been looking forward to greeting you."

They entered the premises and went up the stairs to the private rooms.

"Saturday is not a good day for us." it was her mother speaking after the normal introductions had been completed, "And especially this Saturday, what with the party tonight, and us moving tomorrow, we won't have much time to see you let alone have a chat."

"That's alright Mum, Chris and I thought we would watch the show tonight, kip down somewhere and give you a hand in the morning,"

"There's no place to sleep love, most of the things are packed away anyway."

Liz had put her arm around Christopher's waist. "Mum don't let's worry about it now, we will work something out."

"Yes Mrs 'H', you don't mind if I call you Mrs 'H' do you? In a place this size it will not be a problem to find somewhere to kip down."

Chris, already knew the building was sizeable but when Liz took him around and showed him he was surprised as it was beyond his expectations.

When they got to what used to be her bedroom, now looking neglected and untidy, although the bed was still standing, "There you are, I knew we would find somewhere to sleep."

"I don't think Mother would like that." She had a teasing grin on her face.

"What do you mean?" He was looking at her in horror.

"Sleeping together!" She received a blank look from Chris, so she continued, "Mum's a bit old fashioned and we are not married."

"Oh, the idea of staying the night suddenly doesn't seem so attractive." He was looking solemn, she asked "Would you prefer to get a cab home tonight and come back in the morning?"

"That idea is certainly starting to have a certain amount of attraction."

She laughed and gently punched him on the arm and led him away to show him more of the building.

After leaving the living quarters they arrived on

a wide carpeted area. Liz crossed the area quickly saying, "let me show you the Casino."

As they went into the area, they met a woman who was about to leave. "Hello Carol – just showing Christopher around, although I did not expect to see you as it is a bit early."

Liz turned to Chris "Carol manages the Casino, later on the rest of the staff will arrive."

"Just getting ready for tonight, although right now I am going for a cup of tea before coming back to finishing off."

Further into the space could be seen the various gaming tables.

As Carol went past them to leave the room, Chris asked "I think I am getting the layout of this place – my guess we are somewhere above the Public Bar."

They were leaving the Casino having had a quick look round "Yes you are partly right as part of it is over the Saloon bar." She was smiling at him and holding his hand "Come on these stairs will take us down to the main entrance."

At the bottom of the stairs they pushed their way through double doors into the main lobby of the building.

They arrived to see her father speaking with three men, who stopped talking as Liz and Chris came through the door arm in arm.

"Hi Dad, just showing Christopher around."

"Oh! Liz, come over here and meet Detective Inspector Green, he's from the police." Ignoring the other policeman he continued. "And of course, this is George Pendleton the new manager of The Black Rose"

The pair had walked over hand in hand, "A real live detective, I don't know if I've met one before." Liz was smiling "How do you do, this is my fiancé, Christopher."

The Inspector replied "Yes, we know each other from the bank, don't we Chris?" They were shaking hands as he said it.

"Nice to see you again Inspector, how's your family?"

"They are well..." The policeman just stopped himself asking the same question.

Liz had put her free hand through her father's arm as if to protect him, "What's my father been up to Inspector?"

Although she spoke to the Inspector her eyes were taking in the other policeman they had not been introduced to, who was a little younger and standing a respectful half pace behind his superior.

"The Inspector has called to warn us to be extra careful, after the bombing of the pubs in Birmingham and other places just recently."

"Why this pub, Inspector, have you had some intelligence or something to have the need to have to warn the management?" Chris asked.

"No! Not this pub in particular, we are warning all places of entertainment to be on their guard, we don't know where ... or if they will strike next, although there is the likelihood they will. There is a big flap on to try and prevent any reoccurrence."

Liz looked the senior officer in he eye "What would you like us to do Inspector Green?" she had spoken slowly, as Liz was feeling provocative, her eyes flashed, and she was holding her father a little closer, but her voice had a double meaning.

Suddenly the Inspector felt uncomfortable, he cursed himself, all these years in the force and suddenly he was feeling embarrassed by a slip of a girl who had smiled at him in a knowing way.

He looked away and speaking to her father saying, "I am sure you won't have any problems, Burt."

He quickly glanced at Liz before continuing "You know where we are, if you think something is unusual or anything that's not what it should be, then don't hesitate to give us a call."

Again, he glanced at Liz.

"Yes, thanks Officer for calling round, and as I told you it is my last night here, and we are going to be very busy ... in fact I think we are fully booked, so let's hope there is no trouble."

"Bye, Inspector." Liz waved to him as she started to pull Chris in the direction of the function room, whilst the others went the other way.

"Did you have to do that?" Chris said it almost sharply.

"It was fun wasn't it? ... He almost blushed ... did you see?"

"Poor fellow he didn't know what to do with himself." The double doors swung too behind them as they entered the large room used on Party Nights.

"This is a lovely room, with the high 'A' framed ceiling just fascinating."

"A long while ago this was where the barons used to eat, you can imagine the fires burning down at the end there with the ox being roasted. Although below here is the original old kitchen, which is now part of the cellar complex. The rest of the building is a lot later than this, and was built when it was converted into a home by some wealthy businessman in the past."

"You must have loved living here, so different to normal houses."

"Quite honestly I hated it."

She tugged his hand again, "If we go over there past the stage, we can get into the modern kitchens and then down some very old narrow stairs into the cellars which was the original cooking area."

As they went down the old stone steps into the cellars Liz asked. "Hold my arm Chris, it's so eerie down here."

They stopped at the bottom and looked at the vast area, a row of small wattage naked bulbs hung from the ceiling casting pools of light with dark corners.

"We are standing just below the modern facility, and what you can see is below the function hall, all those arches support the floor, and that's where the old kitchen used to be."

"I had expected to see crates of beer and things." He was looking around him as he said it.

"Oh there is, all that down here, just over the other side there, come on I'll show you."

With that she grabbed hold of his hand and dragged him into the gloom.

"Do you think there are any rats down here, it looks like the perfect place for them to be?"

"Oh Chris don't, I try not to think of things like that." Holding his hand tightly she could not help looking around for any signs of them.

"There you are barrels and barrels of beer, the spirits are kept in a different part."

"Is that what that wire fence is for?" He had nodded in the direction of an enclosure.

"Yes, it is a secure area which cannot be assessed from here you have to go through the bar, it stops the cooks from helping themselves.

"Is that true?" He looked at her in the half light with a questioning look on his face.

"Yeah, before Daddy had this fencing put up, the cooks had their own barrel, there is so much stuff down here that nobody noticed, can you imagine slaving over a hot stove and then disappearing down into the cellars for a quick one."

"A bit uncomfortable I would have thought." he was once again grinning at her admiring her excitement and energy.

"You and your sex drive and you know damn well I meant a drink." She had glared at him

"How many staff does your father employ?"

"Lots, on a busy night there are many 'part timers' which may make the numbers up to as many as twenty five or thirty – I don't really know, and then there's the band on top of that."

"You know, when you have spoken of your pub before I imagined a little bar somewhere, I didn't imagine anything of this size."

He paused before continuing "I can just imagine the cooks coming down and having their own barrel, I wonder how they did it?"

"I think they had it on a stand with a tap on it, they used to cover it up over the other side of the cellar, Dad reckons they were doing it for years."

"Do you think they were reserved for them?" He pointed in the direction of two kegs.

"What are you talking about?" she was looking in the direction he was pointing.

"Those two barrels with the sign 'For Backup Only' do you think they are reserved for the cooks."

"Dad will kill them if they are!" She stopped and looked at the barrels more closely saying "I think they are in the wrong place, as that beer is only sold in the Public Bar."

"If it is important then perhaps, we should go and tell your father as he may want them moved."

She looked at her watch saying, "He'll be on his break - it won't take long for us to move them into the other part of the cellar, where they should be."

"Perhaps your father wanted them put here."

"No, it's those lazy draymen, they just put the kegs wherever they like with no thought of where they should be. Funny though, they have got different seals on them than normal, I'll ask Dad why that is?"

She looked at him "Come on grab hold of the handle on your side and we will have them shifted in no time."

A few minutes later a little out of breath after moving the two heavy kegs, Liz said "Come on love, I'll race you to the steps."

With that her high heels beating a tattoo on the stone floor as she made her way to the stairs, with him following behind.

Detective Inspector Green

After leaving The Black Rose, the Detective Inspector along with his aid visited other concerns to spread the warning of a possible attack, after which they made their way to the police station.

He was still smarting from the look in Liz's eyes, and wondering if she had meant it as a pass or was she playing with her boy friend. He speculated if she knew Chris was married.

The day was starting to get out of hand, he still had a mountain of work to do before he could go home, he hated these flaps, they wasted so much time and stopped him from doing, what he called real police work.

He still could not understand why the powers that be had insisted someone of his rank to do the rounds, instead of a constable, perhaps they thought he would recognise if something was suspicious.

At the station there were a number of queries to sort out before he got to his own office, where he finally settled down to clear the outstanding queries on his desk.

The evening had lost the daylight, so he put on the lights and looking at the clock, and saw it was nearly seven o'clock.

A pile of papers needed his signature, he pulled them to him and started to go through them carefully, signing them and putting them in his out tray.

He started to look at the incident information that had also come in for that day. Slowly and carefully, with his pen in his hand he was going down through the list of items scribbling his initials next to them after reading through them.

When he saw the report from a London Police Station of the missing dray vehicle with its driver and mate. He stopped and thought for a moment and then looking at the clock he realised he was running late, so he acknowledged it, and went on to the next item.

He had arranged to meet some of his detective team in the local public house for a little team bonding, quickly clearing his desk he left the building.

Half an hour later saw him sitting on a bar stool, most of the others had left and gone their separate ways leaving just two sergeants discussing the latest cricket score in from Australia.

When he joined them, they were debating whether England would be able to win the biannual competition for the Ashes Cup and bring it home this season.

As was normal on these occasions, although being involved in the conversation, his mind would go over the day's events.

The meeting earlier in the day concerning the terrorist activities and the attack on two places of entertainment by planting a car bomb outside the venue, not only causing death and injury but also destroying half of the building.

The discussion and what he had learned at the event repeatedly went through his mind, as he had a feeling, he was missing something.

He had already been chided a few times for being deep in thought, more than usual as one of the others put it.

But he was certain there was something during the last period that was important. He was going through the day's events, from the meeting in the morning and then the visit to The Black Rose, he could feel it, something that needed looking into, but he was finding it difficult to understand what it was.

It was his turn to buy a round, he signalled to the barman who was serving at the other end of the bar.

"Sorry for the delay Sir, but one of the barrels has just run out of beer, it won't take long while I change it." The barmen did not wait for a reply but vanished towards the cellar.

D.I. Green looked at the two sergeants, whom he had known his entire police career. They were still talking about cricket. He spoke over their conversation.

"I know you both saw the report concerning the disappearing Brewery lorry from a London Nick as your initials were on it."

"Yeah, it was a bit careless weren't it Governor, what do you think - somebody knew where there was a party that could do with a lot of booze. I can see all the revellers running out into the road with a glass in their hand." He gave a little laugh as he took another mouthful of beer.

"No Byron, you miss the point. I can understand a lorry vanishing, I can understand two fellows going absent, all sorts of reasons for that to happen, but when two fellows disappear with a Brewery lorry, perhaps we should look at that more carefully."

At that point the barman came over and took their order. Byron spoke "Well, what about it and what's on your mind Guv?" He was looking serious.

"About the only people that have access to a pub, without question, are the Brewery people."

"Are you saying that the lorry is nicked so somebody can get into a pub, surely Guv it can't be that simple, surely there are too many checks?"

"My God Dave Logan, you can be so thick sometimes. Let's just suppose these people who have been blowing the front off pubs by planting a car bomb outside want to make a bigger bang and destroy the whole building, not just the front. If you wanted to do a big nasty thing like that, how would you get the explosives into the building?"

Dave was still being obstinate "Come on now ... are you saying they have nicked a lorry so they can blow a pub up ... it's a bit farfetched isn't it Guv?"

"No wait a minute Dave, what the Governor is saying, if you wanted to make a big bang, like he says, then you would need to be able to get into a building with no questions asked, and aren't the draymen the perfect answer, and when you think about it, two of them have disappeared. Why?"

"Christ, I think you could be right." It suddenly occurred to him, his eyes had gone wide as he made the remark,

"Do you think they have held the driver and his mate on ice somewhere and have been delivering bombs, but hold on you two it couldn't be, that was yesterday, surely we would have known by now. And there is another thing Guv, it is nothing to do with us for surely it is the London Nick's problem?" he had a feeling it was going to be a late night.

"You willing to take that chance Dave, how would you feel if one of the pubs on our beat got blown up?"

The Detective Inspector looked at them both as they nodded their heads.

"I think we are in agreement. Byron get on to that Brewery, I don't care who you have got to disturb, I want to know in the next forty five minutes, where that lorry was supposed to be delivering to.....you Dave go with him and give him what help you can, as soon as you find out get in touch with me in my office where I will try and get in touch with the local pubs to see if they had a delivery in the last twenty four hours. If you need any further help tell the Desk Sergeant, I authorised it."

The two officers were already finishing their drinks as the made their way to the door as they did so, putting the glasses down on another table.

The Black Rose

Jane, driving her motor scooter arrived in the car park of The Black Rose at the same time as Pam and Paul, all three excited to get ready for the evenings work.

"Hello you two, how are you both, I bet you are getting eager for tomorrow, you are getting married in the afternoon I believe. I'm surprised you are working tonight."

"There are a few reasons why we needed to get married before the end of this month and that's why we decided on a Sunday wedding, anyway we could not let Burt and Irene down."

The three stood in a group waiting for Jane to park the scooter and get organised.

Paul started talking "Anyway, not only did we not want to let the bosses down tonight, as it will be a great evening, what with the Governor and his Missus leaving, how could we miss that."

They were standing next to Jane watching as she stood her machine on its stand. When that was achieved, she started to un-strap her helmet as they walked towards the entrance to the bars.

"Quite honestly, I would have preferred to have got married today, but Pam would not spend her wedding night working,"

"I should think not, I bet you gave him what for when he suggested it."

Jane had turned to the other woman without waiting for an answer she continued "It looks like we are going to be very busy tonight, the car park is already starting to fill up."

"Yeah, not only is the band superb but the cabaret is also great, come on girls we are going to get wet it's starting to rain again." The three quickened their pace.

Jane asked, "the singer has played here before, hasn't she?"

Pam excitedly said "Wow, what a great singer, last time she sung here people stood up and just went on and on clapping, she is quite funny as well."

Pam changed the subject just as they reached the side door by which the staff entered, "Did you see the story a few days ago about the two pubs that the IRA blew up?"

"That was terrible, Mum nearly wouldn't turn up tonight when she saw that – she didn't want me to go either."

"She is still coming, isn't she? Mum and Dad are looking forward to seeing her again."

"Yes Pam, I talked her back into it again, she was only looking for an excuse not to turn up, she had taken some persuading in the first place. I've ordered her a taxi for in an hour's time, without a doubt she will be here."

The staff were surprised to see the Landlord Burt Hallard dressed in an evening suit with a bow tie

"Hello Burt, you're looking all dressed up this evening, it is a little unusual to see you around at this time." It had been Paul who had spoken, shouting over the heads of the two girls as he held the door open for them.

"Thank you Paul, hello girls, we have a lot to go through could you join the others in the saloon bar before we start, I want to have a word with you all."

They had been the last to arrive and were surprised to see the others were all waiting, standing in little groups talking.

Burt ushered them into a cluster in front of him and raising his voice saying, "If you could all pay attention for a moment, there is something important I want to say."

A hush slowly came over the assembly as they all turned to look at the Landlord. The new Proprietor, who was to take full control as from the next day, stood to one side, with a small smile on his lips that seemed to say tonight you are in charge, but I can wait as from tomorrow it's all mine.

"What I've got to say is a bit sad, as you all know I've been here many years and have made many, many friends."

He had paused and was looking around at their faces, they in turn were gazing back at him each wondering what he was going to say.

"Before I get to the sad part, this evening is going to be slightly different from other occasions in that the Mayor of the City and other dignitaries will be here, I also understand the Managing Director of the Brewery is also coming and that is why we have a table laid out on a dais which is where they will sit."

"Mr Pendleton and myself," He had nodded in the direction of the new Landlord "have been asked by the police to be especially careful this evening, this is following the bombing of the two pubs a short time ago, they think the terrorist may be looking at other targets, although they say it is unlikely for anything to happen."

At first total silence as the members considered what he was saying. This was followed by soft murmuring, which went around the group as they looked from one to the other and finally back to the boss. "Does that mean we have had a warning or something?" It had been one of the waiters who had spoken.

"No, no nothing of the kind." Burt was shaking his head "The police, I understand, are warning the public in general to be on the lookout, and they have also spoken with all the other pubs especially those ones they think could be at risk, we come in that category because of the Army personnel that visit us."

The murmuring got louder. He held up his hands, "Now please, let me finish."

He waited for the group to go quiet, "It is a terrible thing that these people have done, and I think it's only wise that we should be just that bit more careful and keep our eyes open."

"What precautions are there in place, or how are we expected to control somebody throwing bombs about?" It was the same waiter who had spoken before. Silence settled in the room, all were waiting for the answer.

"As I said before there is little risk but we need to be on our guard. So, two things, first we will ban any form of bag, or cases for that matter from coming into the premises."

They all looked at him expectantly "Secondly, and this may be a bit difficult, we will also be asking the ladies to open their handbags when they come in so we can inspect them."

A general murmur went up around the group, "Do you mean we are going to stop every one that comes in?" It was the same waiter who had spoken.

"Yes, I don't see any other way, and I'm sure if we put a sign up saying why we are doing it everybody will understand."

"How are we going to do that Governor?"

"We will close part of the entrance off so that the clients will have to pass a table that we will put there for the purpose, and now I want two people to stand there and check the bags."

"But Governor, what are we checking the bags for, wasn't it a car bomb they used previously?"

"That's true, we will also park our own cars outside the windows to the restaurant and saloon bar, and then those on the door will make sure that no one leaves a car in the car park and disappears".

"Come on boys and girls, let's have a bit of quiet while we work this out. It shouldn't be too difficult, and I'm sure everyone will understand, Mr Pendleton, has agreed to take the door to start the evening, Jack, will you please help him. Everyone else keep your eyes and ears open and if you think someone is acting strangely then please tell Mr Pendleton or myself, that will be all, come on let's get started."

Jack Quincy, who was one of the waiters, and had been there almost as long as the governor himself, waited for the meeting to break up, and made his way to where Burt was standing talking to his replacement.

"What about my tips Burt." He looked him in the face before continuing. "Saturday nights is a good night for me normally." He stood there waiting for an answer a determined look on his face.

Burt looked at George as if to say we don't really need this.

Turning back to the waiter and smiling said "Jack, I want somebody who knows the clients, and I want it to be a person I can trust on the door, what we will have to do is make your money up, will that be alright Jack?"

"Yes, I expect so, will you give that to me in cash, I won't have to pay tax or anything on it will I?"

"No Jack, we will pay you in cash, I wouldn't want you to be out of pocket, come on let's see if we can get the entrance organised."

Frances & Lewis

The Saturday had dragged by. Four o'clock had come and gone. Frances sat in her room waiting. She was dressed as she had been requested in a simple cocktail dress with high heeled shoes, nothing but plain smart clothing so that no one would be able to remember too clearly what she had been wearing,

The front door was being shut and she heard him go into the downstairs room, her heart had started to beat faster. All day she had been rehearsing what she would say to him when she saw him.

Half an hour went past, she was becoming fearful, was she supposed to go downstairs, and if she was keeping him waiting, would he beat her for being late. She tried to reason with herself, surely nobody could be that unkind when all he had to do was shout up the stairs.

Just when she had decided it was time to go down, she heard his heavy feet on the stairs. She found herself almost cowering into the corner, pulling herself together thinking that she would only have to put up with him for a couple of hours and then she would be on her way home.

"You look really smashing." was his comment as he opened the door.

She almost retorted '*That's no thanks to you*'. But letting the impulse pass she attempted a smile and was surprised to find that it didn't come out too bad and replied by saying a simple "Thank you ".

"If you are ready, we will go downstairs and get the timers, and remember be careful with them."

On the journey to The Black Rose she was surprised how he could keep up a steady conversation about normal everyday things. She was busy looking at the outside world which she knew after tonight would seem different to her.

Another thing which surprised her, up until this moment she didn't think she would have any problem in carrying out the mission.

Now, it all seemed so different as the time of reckoning was to hand. She was not certain if she could go through with it.

Although she was sure she had not shown it, but Elisabeth felt a strong sense of revulsion for the man sitting next to her.

As he drove the car towards their destination he was making small talk, but her curt replies and nods made it obvious she was not listening, in the end he said, "You had better put up a better show than you are doing, because we don't want to be remembered as the couple that were arguing all night."

There was no answer; Frances was thinking of her mother and how she was going to tell her she was pregnant.

After the horrors her family had been through it was not fair that she had such terrible news to impart to her.

She started to think of abortions but her whole upbringing would not allow her to consider that form of action for very long.

Her mind was searching for an answer to her predicament, there did not appear to be one. The grip on her knee frightened her, she looked at Lewis, "What's wrong?"

"I've been talking to you, and you have not said a word in reply."

"Oh...I..." She did not know what to say, but she was saved any further need to a reply as he carried on for her.

"I was saying the purpose of the two of us going, is so that it will look like two people happy in each other's company, if you are sulking that's not going to look too good, is it.?"

"No, I don't suppose it is, I'm sorry." Despite herself she found herself apologising.

Frances tried to smile at him but found it difficult. She wanted to be at home she didn't want any more of this nonsense. She wanted to be with her sister and her father, she didn't want to have to go home and tell her mother her latest bad news.

What once seemed noble and right now felt sordid, and terrible, she took another look at her companion and realised what a stranger he was.

He had continued unaware of the thoughts that were racing through her. "Now come on, snap out of it, let's see if we can look the part."

What a beautiful engaging smile he had, but now she knew how sinister that smile could be.

Frances knew she was trembling as he revolted her. How was she going to get through the next few hours she did not know?

But worse - how was she going to be able to live with the knowledge of the carnage she will have helped to create. Surely there was a different answer besides revenge, for revenge sake. Maybe there was another way. Perhaps she would not have to live with the memory.

She hadn't even noticed that they had pulled off the road into a car park, it wasn't until he leaned over to open the door for her did she realise that they had come to a stop, she winced as he reached across her, she looked up quickly, "Oh! We are here."

My God, how was she going to go through with it, her legs were shaking already, and "Do we have to go in for a minute?"

"What's the point in sitting out here?"

"I don't feel very well give it a minute and I'll be alright....while we wait you could point out the layout of the building." Frances was thinking perhaps if she took some deep breaths then it would settle her nerves.

"Alright, if you think it will help." He wiped the windscreen with his gloves as it was starting to mist over.

"Over that side of the building is the public bar, where all the regulars go. Over on the right is where the party will be, it's immediately above the cellars.

What you can't see from here is that the restaurant joins with the public bar at the back of the building. Where the front entrance is there is another bar, from that you go through an arch way which is on the right as you go in." "

He had turned towards her trying to make out her face in the dark looking for some form of acknowledgement; he got a weak smile as a form of reply.

"I cannot understand why you asked the question as you have been here enough times to know the layout." He was still trying to see her with concern on his face.

"Shall we go in?" by way of an answer she opened the car door. They then noticed a taxi pull up at the front entrance and a middle aged lady got out of it and was greeted by one of the staff, what they could not hear was Jane greeting her mother saying "Hi Mum, glad you could make it, come on in, the others haven't arrived yet but I'll show you to a table."

June & Michael

June had been looking forward to the evening with excitement, she was bemused over the fact that in their married life they had only been out to dinner twice.

Now here she was going out again, only because she had agreed with her husband's desire on meeting this other couple and changing partners. The result, they were going out to eat for the second time in as many months.

She had spent the afternoon in the hairdressers, and now she stood in front of the long mirror in the bedroom, getting dressed for the evening.

She had bought sexy underwear in red, and as she slipped the last clip into place she looked good, and better still, she felt first-class.

She was just slipping the new dress over her head, which she had also bought for the occasion, when Michael came out of the bathroom, "My, you look somewhat nice."

"Thank you kind Sir, but only 'somewhat?'" She smoothed the dress down over her thighs, twisting her arms up her back to manipulate the zip.

He was tucking a towel around his waist adding "It's a nice thought if that is for me."

"Of course, it is Darling." She turned and kissed him very gently on the lips, "who else would it be for?"

He knew she was teasing, but that did not matter, he could not remember the last time that she had looked so lovely, or so happy.

Slipping his arms around her, she gently pushed him away, "No, please don't, you'll spoil my make up, and it took simply ages to do." She ducked under his arm and left the room. Michael felt rejected as she swept down the stairs.

Turning to the wardrobe he selected his outfit for the evening and ten minutes later he finally followed his wife to find her waiting in the lounge a drink in one hand, she waved at the bottle, "Would you like one, darling?"

He looked longingly at the glass and shrugging his shoulders saying "No, I had better not - I'm driving."

"You are ready then?" June was looking in her handbag making sure she had everything, as she said it.

He was picking up the car keys "Yes, of course, I'm bloody ready."

He was regretting their involvement with the other couple and would have much preferred to stay at home and watch the football.

"You don't have to talk to me in that tone, love."

"It's just that you look so lovely and I have a feeling it is not for me, anyway there is a good game on the telly this evening."

Opening the door for him and with a smile on her face "You and your bloody football - anyway wouldn't you want me looking lovely?"

"Well you have never gone to that trouble before, have you – it looks like it could rain , had better get the brolly?" they had arrived out in the short drive and he was looking up at the sky.

June was walking around to the far side of the car and looking at him across the bonnet "You have hardly taken me out before, but never to a restaurant like tonight, with a dance and cabaret, it's going to be great fun." She glared at him "and now you are trying to spoil it saying you would prefer to watch football."

"Of course, I'm not, I want you to be happy and I am looking forward to the evening just like you are."

"Why's that? She was looking at him with a grin and added "so you can get your hands in Kay's knickers?" She was leaning over and opening the car door.

"You can speak about knickers, as I understand it you could not wait to get yours off the last time – or perhaps you are not wearing any."

"Would you like to see?" They were sitting in the car and teasingly she started to slowly lift her skirt, before pulling it down and laughing.

Not a great deal more was said in the car, she was feeling very happy and looking forward to the evening.

While Michelle drove he was wondering what he had let himself in for. He had thought he would try and liven up his sex life with this swapping idea, he didn't think June would enjoy it, let alone want to do it again.

He glanced at her perhaps she was teasing him, getting her own back because he had suggested it in the first place.

"Let's make this the last time, aye love?"

"Last time for what?" She said coyly, feeling her nipple going taught at the thought of how the evening was going to develop.

"You know what I mean, this free love thing, you looking nice and going with another man, I'm not certain if I want to go through with it again."

"Well, I suppose we could all have dinner and then go home. What will you say to Dennis? I can't help remembering what Kay said to me before breakfast the last time that you were big and strong - she will be very disappointed."

She smiled at him and he knew the evening would follow the same pattern as before

"That's just girl talk." He said a little sharply. "I suppose we could just turn round and go home."

"What and watch football, also cheating me out of my night out. Cinderella is in her coach and she is going to the ball, how you work it out from there is your problem."

Not much more was said on the remainder of the journey, and their timing was such that they turned into the car park of The Black Rose, just behind the couple they were going to meet.

Parking the two cars together, they exchanged greetings with the two men kissing the ladies on the cheek. Dennis could not resist holding June's bottom before the four strolled towards the entrance.

Michael's heart went into overdrive when he first saw Kay. His eyes wandered over her taking in the very short light blue hot pants belonging to a play suit with long boots and tights, the swell of her breasts at the top. He knew he was stuttering when they made their greetings.

Jack, standing at the door recognised Dennis and his wife, "Good evening Mr & Mrs Langton....nice to see you again" he nodded is head at the other two. "We are sorry about the security arrangements, but the management feel it's the best in the circumstances, after the previous outrages."

"Why Jack, are you expecting any trouble?" Dennis was holding June's hand tightly as if to stop her running away.

"No Sir, we have been advised along with every other premises of entertainment to take extra care in the next few weeks." It had been the replacement Landlord who had replied to Dennis's question.

The party had gone quiet and edgy at the implications of the security check, brightened up with the reassurance that was given and at the request of an embarrassed Jack, the two ladies opened their bags for a quick look by the staff, who were also showing signs of awkwardness.

Dennis tried to break the atmosphere that had developed, "You are not very busy tonight?"

"I think you are a little early, Sir." He shut June's bag and added, "We are fully booked, it should be a good evening."

Dennis took June's arm as they left the check in. Michael seeing this action took hold of Kay's hand and chatting as if they had never been a part in the past few weeks.

They made their way over and sat at a table near the bar, to order an aperitif, before giving their order for dinner, and taking their table in the restaurant.

Michael could not help feeling there was something more happening between his wife and Dennis. He could not quite understand what it was, it was something to do with the way they seemed to be comfortable in each other's company, and guessed they were seeing each other at other times, he made a mental note to ask her later.

Frances & Lewis

As they approached the door to the Restaurant, they saw that other women were having their handbags inspected. Frances' heart started to beat faster, not knowing what to do.

Lewis took hold of her hand saying "We had better go back to the car, when we get there open the door and leave the items in it. Don't take too long as we don't want them to get suspicious, I want them to think we have forgotten something."

As they were on the verge to turn and go back, they saw the table being removed and people were being let in again without any inspection.

Inside the entranceway four couples had reacted badly to the need of the ladies having to have their bags inspected and had refused to go in and had left in a huff.

George Pendleton, the new Landlord, realised it was upsetting the clients and decided to stop the intervention, so the access to the premises returned to normal.

Jack murmured that he had always thought, that not only had it all been a waste of time, but it upset his customers as well.

As Lewis and Frances entered the property, the table was still being put to one side by a couple of waiters, and the restriction of the silk red cord which had been in place to create a single walkway, was being removed.

Jack was saying "Good evening, it is nice to see you again, you are becoming quite the regulars."

Lewis replied, "Thank you, we come for the wonderful cooking, and the steaks are just perfect." Frances was nodding her head.

As they walked away Jack was looking at the new manager "I did not know they were Irish, perhaps we should have waited a bit longer."

"Yes, I know what you mean, but we can't be suspicious of people just because of their nationality."

"Yes, I agree with you, but I have been watching them recently and they do not seem to be very comfortable in each other's company."

The Army

A dark green coloured minibus with Army logos came into the car park coming to a stop outside the main entrance, a few of the new arrivals stepping to one side as it came to a stop.

A smartly dressed soldier who had been driving, quickly went around the vehicle and opened the sliding door to one side.

The first person out was an upright officer dressed in his mess uniform including a highly polished Sam Brown Belt and as the colonel stepped onto the sidewalk the driver stood to attention and saluted, which the officer acknowledged.

There were a further four officers each leaving the minibus after which they helped their wives out and arm in arm entered The Black Rose.

The women dressed in long evening gowns giving a splash of colour to the group.

All of the men were dressed in uniform displaying their various statuses with medals, pips or crowns on their shoulder epaulets.

The driver who had driven the vehicle, parked it where he would wait for the others to finish their evening entertainment.

Standing in the doorway to greet them were Burt and Irene, along with the new Landlord, as they stood in a group there were introductions all round, the conversation was light and easy with soft laughter and giggles as they exchanged small talk.

Terry Parks was hovering around and as the conversation started to settle, he told them it would be a little while before their dining table was ready.

The colonel replied in a deep voice "Never mind son, we will make ourselves comfortable here in the lounge." Pointing to a group of tables as he said it.

Frances & Lewis

Most of the seats had been taken in the lounge, so Frances and Lewis were sitting on bar stools a little way from where the Army had made themselves comfortable.

Both were sipping from a slim glass while they waited for their table in the main room of the building.

The Martini was helping her to calm down as the conversation between them was strained. He was trying to make her relax "Did I tell you, you look lovely?"

It was not the thing she wanted to hear and murmured "I think so, in fact a few times - how long do you think the table will be?" All she wanted to do was to get the evening over with.

"Relax" He put is hand on hers "the waiter said it would not be too long."

They sipped their drinks, most of the time Frances was looking at the floor, she was longing to sit down at a table where she wouldn't feel so conspicuous.

A little way along the bar was a group of well dressed men, although a little brash with bright ties and plenty of gold about their person, bracelets and the like. All were enjoying the gentle banter between each other.

Frances looked up at them with envy, as they were so relaxed as if they did not have a care in the world.

She could not help wondering what they were celebrating and wished she could join them and unite in their laughter.

Instead she was here on a mission to destroy and kill.

They appeared to be such nice people, so different from the thing she was with and she had an aversion not to hurt them. The thought crossed her mind that perhaps she should warn them?

Her reverie came to an end when one of them speaking loudly said "Come on Harry drink up, let's get up stairs and get the game started – I saw Calvin going up there just now."

She smiled to herself as they left, taking their laughter with them, the room felt a little empty without them.

She looked over at the well dressed men in Army uniform. They also seemed relaxed and enjoying the evening.

Frances could feel the hatred inside her, what right did they have to be here enjoying themselves, after what they did to her father and sister.

The vision of them both, as she last saw them, came vividly to mind and the need for revenge came to the fore.

"Who are all these other people....I didn't expect there would be so many." She had returned her gaze to Lewis.

He was starting to get warning signals about the stability of his companion, he answered so as not to upset her,

"All part of the Army, and as you can see they have the blue flying wings insignia on the shoulders." And then he tried to change the subject, "We will go in, in a minute, the waiter is coming this way, no doubt to take our order."

The waiter came up to them smiling with a notebook in his hand. After a brief discussion they gave their meal orders and then followed him into the restaurant where he seated them at a table.

As they walked between the various tables, Frances was aware of the two transmitters in her bag, it felt to her that everyone was looking at her pointing at what she was carrying.

She looked about her and was relieved to see everyone intent on chatting and laughing, and no one was looking at her or taking any notice as they walked past.

She wanted to join them, she had had enough of the reason why they were they were there.

"Will you do it.?" They were seated at the tables opposite each other with its sheer white covering, she had leaned forward and whispered the request to him.

"Don't be a bloody fool, how the hell are you going to pass them to me without anyone seeing them, and that is why they are with you, nobody takes any notice of a woman looking in her bag. Just do what you have been taught to do."

He was getting worried as he was not sure she was stable enough to do what was needed and was starting to think of abandoning the whole operation.

"Yes, you are right." She stammered sitting back at the onslaught of his whispered words.

The Black Rose

Bernard, the newspaper seller, had arrived accompanied by Pam and Paul's mother and father. Jane helped in getting them seated on the same table as her mother Ivy. As they sat down one of them in the group was saying I do like it here, it is so nice and relaxing, and the food is wonderful.

Ivy was not too certain, she was not used to fussy food, a plate of chips would suit her. Not knowing what to say she started to look around her as was her way, taking in events and people.

Her eyes settled on Frances a few tables away. She got up and went over to her. Resting her hand on her shoulder she said, "You alright dear, you don't look very well?"

Lewis, who had watched her making her way to their table, was shocked *did this person know them?* He was a little relieved to realise it was some busy body trying to comfort his partner who he had to admit did look pale.

He answered for her "She has a toothache." He was saying the first thing that came into his head.

"Oh dear, that is terrible, would you like some pain killers, I have got some here somewhere?" As she was saying it she was searching through the white shoulder bag. Frances almost blushed at the word killers.

"No, it is alright we have just come from the dentist and he has given her some." Lewis was getting desperate he needed to get rid of this woman.

"Oh dear" was Ivy's response, rubbing Frances's shoulder "I hope it gets better, you don't want it spoiling your evening." Smiling at Lewis she turned round and went back to her table.

Frances felt trapped '*could she really go through with it, set the two bombs, and then get up and walk out of here and leave all these people to their fate?*'

He was smiling at her again, but his voice was saying different things, "Will you please start smiling as if you are enjoying the evening. We have a little time to go as yet, and we don't want another busy body phoning for a doctor or something."

"You haven't told me what time the plane goes? I want to go back home to Ireland." She was staring at him.

"Could we talk about something different, we are supposed to be a happy young couple."He was smiling at her and took hold of her hand.

"You want me to pretend we are going on our honeymoon, and you haven't told me what time the plane leaves. But I want to know, so please tell me what time does it go?"

Frances didn't like the look in his eyes, there was that funny gleam in them that she had noticed the afternoon of the beating. "We are catching a plane, aren't we?" she said with a look of concern on her face.

"Be careful what you are saying, you don't know who could be listening."

"The nearest table is four feet or more away and I can't hear what they are saying, so I'm sure they can't hear what we are saying, please answer me?"

"There's a change of plans." She looked at him with a surprised look on her face, her eyes wide "Why wasn't I told?"

"There was no need for you to know." He wasn't looking at her and was looking around the room.

"What are the new plans...what are we doing when we leave here?" Her voice had risen, she was feeling cheated.

"Keep your voice down. It is nothing to worry about we are going to my place, and we will leave for Ireland tomorrow."

Her face went red, she remembered what his mother had said about the girl she had to go and attend to. The story of the whip, horror swept through her at the thought of being shut away with this madman. She sat there shaking her head.

~~~

In the Public Bar the party was getting underway and all the regulars had turned up. Hidden in the corner, with a towel over it, was the present they had clubbed together to buy.

The music was blaring out of the speakers on the juke box, which had been set to play continually and most of those present were singing along to some of the old favourites that were being played.

Cheering and raising their glasses, if some beer spilled out it did not matter, what did matter was having fun and planning when they were going to present the Governor and his missus with their gift.

~~~

June, with her husband and their friends, had been seated to one side of the room near to the band, which made conversation a little difficult because of the closeness of the music, although all four of them were in a great mood.

Any fear Michael had shown earlier of this arrangement for dinner and the planned evening ahead, had disappeared when Kay started to run her stocking leg against his.

Exhilaration in him was such he had visions of him laying her on the table and having his way. He grinned to himself at the thought. Prior to that he had not liked the way his wife was looking longingly at Dennis, although jealous, he could not help feeling excitement for the sexual pleasure she would enjoy later.

Detective Inspector Green

In the centre of Guildford at the main Police station for the area, Detective Inspector Green was in his office. First, he needed to confirm with the London 'Nick,' which had filed the report, what action he in Guildford intended taking.

He finally got through to the duty officer and explained his thoughts. The reply was not what he expected "Inspector Green, I cannot agree with you, we have already looked into the missing lorry thoroughly and we do not see any connection with what you are suggesting - so a couple of guys go missing and twenty fours later you are connecting it to some terrorist plot.

I think what you are suggesting is over the top and we will not be involved."

"Are you telling me after the events of the past few weeks when Public Houses have been targeted, you cannot see a connection with a dray lorry going missing and the possibility it could be to do serious damage to some property?"

"Hold on a moment, let me get the file." The phone went dead and it was a few minutes later when he resumed the conversation "As I said, we looked into the disappearance and the officer who dealt with it, is off duty, but looking at his notes he could not see anything suspicious. So as I previously said, I think you are looking for something which is not there."

Detective Inspector Green felt irritated he also needed this person's agreement for him to investigate an event which was out of his area. "I hear what you say but I have a funny feeling about this, and I need your approval for my team to look into it." He could hear the deep breath on the other end of the line.

"Detective Inspector, you must do as you think fit, I will be making a note of this conversation. I wish you well and hope you are not wasting valuable time."

The connection was closed, thinking to himself 'why *did he have to be so difficult he could have just said 'we will give you all our support'?*"

With a deep sigh he picked up the phone and started to try and find on a Saturday night the Directors of the Brewery to ask them to speak to the staff about the destination of the dray.

A little time later he returned to the Incident Room and he was in time to hear Byron shout "At last."

He looked around and saw they had followed his instructions and there were four other officers helping with the phones, all of whom looked up waiting for an explanation. He held his hand over the mouthpiece, saying "I have finally found someone at their home who was on duty at the Brewery when that dray disappeared."

He went back to the conversation "Can I have your name please?"

"Thank you, Margaret,' my name is Sergeant Byron Smith, I am with the Guildford Police Force in Surrey. We understand one of your drays did not come back, can you tell me what happened and what steps were taken yesterday, when the vehicle did not return."

They could hear the murmur of another voice coming from the receiver. "So what you are telling me is you shut up shop and went home, but not before you informed the local Police Station."

From the phone they could hear further murmuring before the policeman continued "Thank you for your help so far – now can you tell me what route the vehicle was taking?" He leant over and pressed a switch on the phone and the speaker attached to it came alive, and the reply boomed across the room.

"I'm not too sure as we give the drivers their route and get on with the next one, and there are many of them on a Friday as all the pubs need deliveries before the weekend."

"Now take your time and see if you can remember." Byron looked up at his colleagues shrugging his shoulders.

"Honestly, I can't remember, it's not something I deal with personally. It would be better if you were to talk to Ted, he knows everything about the drivers and their journeys."

Byron was feeling exasperated but tried not to show it "Thank you Margaret, so my understanding is that you work in the dispatch department with a man called Ted, and he is the person who organises the routes for the men to go on. Do you have Ted's full name?"

"Er...I think it is Walters, he lives somewhere in Bermondsey but frequently goes to his mother's house in Essex over the weekends, well that is what he tells everyone." As she was speaking Dave grabbed a telephone directory off a shelf and started to thumb through the pages under 'W' looking for a Ted Walters.

"One more thing Margaret is his name Ted, or would it be a shortening for Edward?"

There was a temporary halt before she answered "I honestly don't know I have only known him as Ted, and I cannot think of anyone else calling him anything else. Can I go now, my friends are waiting for me to go out?"

"We would prefer it if you were to stay there for a little longer as we may need to talk to you again. Thank you for your help so far." There was a 'ting' as the connection was broken.

The Black Rose

Brian and Sarah arrived and were shown to their table and waited patiently for their guests to get there, and were disappointed when Ken Williams arrived with a woman he introduced as his sister, and explained the others were sorry but at the last minute a family problem precluded them from coming.

The two hosts looked at each other, not only in disappointment but wondering at the continued absence of their benefactor and now doubting if there was one.

As far as Williams was concerned, he did not want them to meet with his Boss and had not passed the invitation on.

With a lot of laughter, the Army were vacating their seating arrangement in the lounge and were being shown to their chairs at a long dining table at the opposite end of the room to the stage.

The exception was the Colonel, smartly dressed in his uniform with all his regalia on display and his wife in a long blue evening gown were.

Jack who had been relieved at the door, and who also thought it had been a total waste of time, was helping Terry Parks and taking orders at the tables.

As the restaurant was now full, the community were wondering why there was one table, on a raised area in a prominent position, which was still not occupied, and who were the expected important individuals to be seated there?

Lewis was feeling good and thinking this operation was going to be even better than they had thought, with dignitaries in the building when it is was wiped out.

Frances, on the other hand was terrified at the thought of going back to his flat, especially after the event of destroying the place they were in, killing and maiming the people who she could see all around her, laughing and enjoying themselves.

Somehow, she had to think of a reason not to go with him.

From the extensive kitchens of the property, dinner was being served throughout the restaurant. Paul in the band had changed the music into a soft melody during this period and as Pam was busy serving at the tables, they still found time to smile at each other.

Chris and Liz were sitting at the same table with Paul and Pam's parents all six were in light hearted conversation which included Jane's mum and Bernard. Ivy who on arrival had been very tense was relaxing and was starting to enjoy herself

Detective Inspector Green

Sergeant Byron had rung off from the girl informing her to stay where she was as a police constable would call on her to take a written statement. In the meantime, the other officers present were thumbing through the telephone directory for South

London looking for a Ted Walters who Christian name could possibly be shown as Edward.

The few which were found the information was shared with Byron and the others, and each had started to call the various numbers to see if they could trace the one they were looking for, who was a dispatcher at the Brewery.

The Inspector had called in more officers to widen the search, one of whom was looking up the names of Walters who lived in Essex.

Inspector Green then started again to try and track down the Managing Director of the Brewery, only to be told he was away for the weekend and could not be contacted.

It was Dave Logan who finally found the Ted Walters family home, the phone was answered by a soft sounding voice and he immediately knew he was talking to what sounded like a young girl who turned out to be the daughter. After questioning her he discovered the address where her father had gone and the phone number.

The Black Rose

A murmur of voices went around the restaurant, as the new and old Landlords, accompanied by the Colonel walked to the main entrance chatting, one was consulting his wristwatch.

Two Police Motorcyclists arrived outside in the main road and held up the traffic to allow a shiny black limousine, with the local authority pendant fluttering from the roof, to sweep into the car park and pull up in front of the main entrance.

Two elderly gentlemen left the vehicle each turning to help their wives out who were dressed in long evening gowns.

They entered the building where they were met by the group who had prepared to greet them. They all stood in a cluster chatting whilst they were being served with an aperitif by the Jack waiter.

At a signal from Burt, Paul gave a roll on the drums as the party entered the restaurant, a few people recognising the new arrivals clapped as they made their way to the table.

~~~

In the Public Bar the party was in full swing, with plenty of alcohol being consumed.

Tee shirt was at the bar ordering another round when the pump ran dry, the barman apologised and as he disappeared towards the cellar he heard the customer saying 'they would sell more beer if they were organised.'

On arriving in the cellar he went to change the barrel and saw the fitting on the keg was different, in fact when he really thought about it the barrel itself looked totally different from the others. What he did not know, the different fitting was the primer to explode the bomb.

He was in a hurry and was not prepared to work out how the different fitting on the keg worked and pulled another into position to resume the flow of beer to the bar.

Detective Inspector Green

In the Incident Room at the Police Station, there was a low hub of voices as the team of detectives went about trying to trace where the dray had been heading, when it disappeared.

The Inspector who could feel there was something seriously wrong about the missing vehicle, was relieved when one of the Constables shouted above the general noise, 'I have located Ted Walters he is at a Caravan park in Thorpe Bay in Essex.'

Green went over to the desk where the information had come from, the Policeman passed him a slip of paper with the details on, he was also told "I have got the local force going there to find him."

The Inspector nodded his head "Get back to them and tell them this is very urgent, we need to know where the dray that went missing, was going and we need a list of the pubs it would have called on. Make sure they understand we need to know, not soon as possible but now."

Frances

The girl from Ireland was in a dilemma, no matter what the Army had done to her family she could not go through with what was being asked of her. One thing was certain she was not going to go with this sadist sitting next to her.

She heard him talking to her but was not listening, fear swept through her, she could not allow him to get near her again, her body still hurt from the last time.

If he was right, then in a few hours time there was no choice but to be at his mercy.

With little thought, Frances moved her hand the few inches to the controls on the timer and turned them to set, at the same time reducing the delay below the twenty minutes, not certain why or by how much.

She knew by her instructions that the bombs would now be armed and there was only a button to press and they would explode. Now it would not be fifteen minutes but a lot less. She didn't care she would sit and wait for the explosion and he would be no more.

He had seen her move her hands, but had thought little of it, the smile that had come over her lips he mistook for one that was in agreement with him.

"Frances, that's a lot better, you are looking a lot happier - we will have our meal and then do what we have to do and go."

There was no need to speak, she just nodded her head and watched as the waiter arrived and started serving their food.

She glanced at the clock, if she continued to the next stage then she would have some time, although now reduced, to decide whether to stay here and die with everyone else, including the thing next to her, or leave and be at his mercy. She was leaning to the former.

What she did not realise was she had been smiling ever since she had made the connection; Frances looked around the room, wondering how many would escape, although knowing in her heart she would not be able to do it. But what were the alternatives?

He couldn't believe his good fortune, she had obviously enjoyed the beating as she was more relaxed since he had told her of the new plans. Perhaps he had found somebody to share his sadistic pleasures, he was starting to get excited just thinking of the remainder of the evening.

~~~

Over the far side of the room nearer to the band, June was saying "I am not really hungry" and pushed the plate of half eaten food to the side.

Michael sitting across the table to her said "That's not like you – you feeling alright?"

"Yes, I'm fine, it's just that the music is too loud and the air is a little stuffy and...well, just and." In reality all she wanted to do was quell the excitement in her stomach by being close to this man sitting next to her.

Dennis looked at her "Perhaps we should go outside for a breath of fresh air, would that make you feel better?" She nodded her head in agreement and they got up together saying they would not be long and left the room. The other two looked at each other in amazement.

Kay, who would have preferred leaving as well was a little disappointed when Michael commented how good the music was, and they could catch up with the other pair a little later.

Detective Inspector Green

It was with relief when the Detective Inspector was told they had located the dispatcher from the Brewery and he was being interviewed.

He paced the floor waiting for the details. A few minutes were to pass when he was given a list of where the dray was to deliver to. "Sir, it's first delivery was in Croydon after which it made its way south and on to Guildford where its final delivery was at The Black Rose."

Unexpectedly for the Detective Inspector the thing which had been bothering him, and now it all fitted into place. It was Party Night at The Black Rose with senior officers of the Army's Parachute Regiment in attendance.

The Inspector was picking up a telephone and dialling for the duty officer at the same time, he raised his voice "Everybody get down to The Black Rose and get everyone to evacuate the building. You will find some uniform officers there, get them to help you. The Mayor is also in attendance with other dignitaries, get them out and for God's sake be quick and be careful."

He pointed to one of the last officers to leave, "Before you go, get on to the Fire Brigade and tell them we have on good authority there is a bomb at The Black Rose, and ask them to be in attendance. After which get on to the Army bomb disposal Unit and tell them the same thing."

The Black Rose

A man and a woman sitting at a table, who, was part of the security for the Mayors party, were astonished to see June and Dennis leave in the middle of the cabaret and made a note of it.

June and Dennis were surprised to see two Police Officers standing outside the front of The Black Rose, not realising they were part of the security for the Mayor.

June held out her hand saying "It is raining - not much but I think we should sit in the car, otherwise we could get wet."

They had walked away from the entrance to the Black Rose when Dennis said, "I have a far better idea – why don't we go home to my place?"
Nodding her head she looked back at the building as if to say what about those two, he added "they can follow when they are ready."

She tightened her grip on his hand and looked up at him "No blue movies then, just a mirrored bedroom." Her eyes were sparkling as she looked at him.

"Maybe a little drink first, but certainly no need for a film, you excite me more than a film can ever do." A short time later Dennis and June arrived back at his house and were frantically getting each other's clothes off as soon as they entered the lounge.

~~~

In the Public Bar the party was continuing, and it was difficult to speak above the noise. The volume had been turned up on the juke box and the deep base beat of the rhythm echoed through the room.

The telephone on a shelf at one end of the bar started to drone, with its insistent ringing which was also relayed in other parts of the building. Before anyone else could respond to it, one of the part time barmen was near the instrument and answered it.

"Hello, this is The Black Rose." One of the revellers tapped him on the shoulder demanding to be served saying "I've been waiting ages for a drink."

He also heard someone speaking but found it difficult to hear clearly above the noise. "Hold on a minute, someone needs serving" he put the receiver down on the ledge without ringing off.

The desk Sergeant, who had been given instructions to telephone and to warn them to clear the premises as the Police suspected an explosive device was in the building. He done as he had been ordered and continued to sit at his desk waiting for someone to pick up the phone again, in the meantime all he could hear was loud music and even louder shouting and laughter.

~~~

The patrons in the Restaurant had started to relax as the harmony of the stage show had started. A female artist in a long red dress was singing a popular song as she stood next to a grand piano, which was being played by a male pianist dressed smartly in a white jacket. To the rear Paul was softly keeping to the rhythm on the drums. Above the noise of the music and the chatter of the people in the distance the wailing of a siren could be heard.

While the cabaret was in progress, the waiters had withdrawn so that the patrons could enjoy the show. Burt and his wife were sitting with the Mayor's party.

Near to the centre of the room the group from the Women's Institute were enjoying themselves and looking forward to the presentation of the award to their most senior member Doris, who was clapping and singing along with the recitalist on the stage.

The people on a table close by, who could not hear the singer clearly, told her to be quiet. The group looked at each other, shrugged their shoulders and refrained from singing along with the artist, who was also relieved when they stopped.

At the police station the duty Sergeant gave up trying to ring The Black Rose as nobody was picking up the instrument to talk to him. In the bar the barman had forgotten about the phone, as he, with another, was very busy looking after customers. When he did remember and picked it up, it was dead.

The conversation at the Bar Games table had lightened up, Ken Williams was being his charming self. Sarah and Brian were not too certain about the relationship he had with the woman, he had called her his sister, as they seemed too close for that, but none of that mattered. Although they found it strange and it raised further suspicions in their minds, as to his true intent.

Kay and Michael who were sitting at the next table were very quiet listening to the music, each curious of where the other two were, although in their minds they guessed they had gone somewhere to be by themselves. June's husband was regretting ever suggesting about going with another couple and also was annoyed with himself for making the original arrangement.

From where Frances was sitting in the Restaurant, she could see through the saloon bar when the double doors to the restaurant were frequently opened, and beyond, part of the car park. It was the flash of car headlights that caught her eye, and in the brief moment she saw it, she was certain it was a police car as there was a blue light on its roof.

It came to her in a flash the previous noise of a siren and now a police car arriving outside the premises. Her upbringing and the church's teaching was prominent in her mind and she knew she could not press the button. She would always regret it and the thought of hurting the old lady who had earlier on had been so caring. No she could not do it.

Lewis had also seen the police car and now there were more sirens, which were becoming louder as they got closer and he realised they had to escape. He leant over to Frances saying "We have got to go, quick set the timer and let's get out of here."

Frances shook her head "No, I can't! And I will not do it!" She crossed herself as the thought of the mayhem her action would create swept through her, as she took solace in her teachings and upbringing.

He pushed her to one side grabbing her handbag quickly finding the timers, she was trying to stop him, but he managed to press a button on one of the units. She was resisting him from pressing the second button. The sharp steak knife was still on his plate waiting to be cleared in the interval. With her free hand she picked it up and forcefully stabbed him in the neck. His blood spurted from the wound creating a red scar across the white dining cloth, and her clothing. He buckled at the knees, grabbing hold of the table to stop himself from falling only to pull the blood stained white material, with the plates, to the floor with a crash, the knife still sticking out of his neck.

The noise of him falling and a chair going over at the same time, brought the attention of the others in the room. Frances pushed the table out of the way and getting to her feet she started to make her way quickly towards the exit. She was aware of the blood on her and was striding across the room, pushing people out of the way. Patrons were standing up and some were screaming, the singer in time honoured fashion continued singing.

The two plain clothes security people , who had been sitting at one of the tables, got up and went over to the dais and after whispering to one of the Mayors party, the two moved to one side as the others all stood up to depart.

The room erupted into confusion when the dignitaries got up to leave. Although no one knew what was going on, but the sight of all the blood and a dead man was enough for people wanting to get as far away as possible.

The band had stopped performing, the singer standing with her hand to her mouth staring into the room. The Army got up from their table and were ushering their wives towards the door

Frances had reached the exit and was pushing through it, the two Policemen who had been stationed outside the building, were coming in from the other direction and collided with her. She shouted at them "There is a bomb under the building, and it is about to explode."

One of the Army officers heard what she said and turned around and shouting told everyone to get out. None of this could be heard in the Public Bar as the merriment continued.

Frances was taken by the arm and passed over to Byron the detective sergeant, who had been the first to arrive. He led her out to one of the police cars asking her if she knew where the bomb was.

Her answer was drowned out by the bomb detonation.

The epicentre of the explosion was below the Public Bar, the stone floor burst upwards, the stone walls in the cellar were blown aside and the fabric of that part of the building collapsed inwards, destroying totally the roof above it as it collapsed inwards, to some also degree part of the Restaurant near to the stage and also part of the Saloon Bar

~~~

The following morning June and Dennis finally got out of bed where they had spent a night of passion. They were surprised to find the house empty and assumed that Kay and Michael had gone to his home.

Over breakfast Dennis put on the television and the first picture they saw was one of The Black Rose and the damage caused to it.

They looked at each other as if they were looking at a stranger, the love and the passion of the previous night a poor ugly memory. June burst into tears.

The Guildford Echo

Sunday 14th April

Terrorist Kill many in Bomb Horror
The Black Rose destroyed in Explosion

By our local reporter:
Last evening, the well known Black Rose Public House and Restaurant, was partly destroyed when terrorists detonated a bomb, which we understand was in the cellars, and completely demolished one of the bars and the Casino also other parts of the building.

There have been many casualties, mainly limited to the Public Bar, which was full at the time, it is not known at this time how many people have been slaughtered.

It is reported that the centre of the explosion took place below this part of the building. Rescue workers are still at the scene and will know the extent of fatalities later today.

We understand that the Landlord Mr Burt Hallard his wife Irene and their daughter are safe, as is the Mayor and other dignitaries, they were all in the restaurant at the time, and that part of the building survived with little damage.

The well liked and popular current possessor of the property was due to be replaced today by a Mr George Pendleton, who we understand died when he went to the Public Bar to warn people of the terrible event, which was about to unfold.

There is also concern for the people who were playing in the Casino which was immediately above the Public Bar which has also been destroyed.

An eye witness to the incident, Paul, who was playing the drums in the band, has told us, the owners of Bar Games, a Mr Brian Roberts and his wife, who were sitting with another couple, did not survive when part of a wall they were sitting near collapsed on top of them, which also killed another couple, only known as Kay and Michael, who were at a nearby table.

In the same instance a Mr Christopher Perkins, a well known local Bank Manager was injured as he was walking past the same area, and is in intensive care at the hospital..

According to reports they were the only casualties of persons who were in the restaurant, when the blast happened.

A Police informer has told us, 'the Police have arrested a young Irish woman who has admitted to being partly responsible for the explosion'. We are further informed she has been charged with murder, although our reporter has been told, she is helping police with their enquiries over other incidents and other arrest have been made.

Detective Inspector Green who is in charge of the Incident Room will be making a statement later today detailing the event and the number of dead and injured.

Late news: We understand the Electricity Board are investigating 'Harry's Car Lot' over the misuse of electricity. They are keen to speak to the owner but it is feared he died in the explosion at The Black Rose

Late news: It is reported the police are looking at what is suspected as fraud at a local bank.

Percychatteybooks
Story Telling (R)
Somerset House
6070 Birmingham Business Park
Birmingham
B37 7BF
Registered Number 2299335

Produced and published in the Hondon Valley, Southern Spain

www.ingramcontent.com/pod-product-compliance
Lightning Source LLC
Chambersburg PA
CBHW072219170626
46813CB00003B/1002